MW00874075

Short

Stories

by

Shreya Goel

Cover art by Shreya Goel

Table of Contents

X Marks the Suspect.... 5

Just Fly.... 33

Like Gold.... 87

Another Lovely Home.... 111

Influenced.... 135

The Same Sweet Home.... 167

The Choice I Make.... 187

4

X Marks the

Suspect

There I was, seated on the steps of our porch, watching the sunset fade behind the house across from ours. The sky immediately darkened as our neighboring house seemed to absorb the light. Then, the innocent wind blew across the window shutters and they created creaky noises. The boards hung on to the windows by nails started to click! click! click!

"Nora!" a voice yelled. I jerked my head towards my sound, looking up at my mother next to me. "Come in, it's getting dark," she said. I gave a sigh to myself and an eye roll before following her inside with a final stare towards the house across from ours.

"How many times do I have to tell you to leave that house alone?!" my mother blurted out, her stern eyes being unable to pinch into my soul.

"I'm sorry, it's just, that house is mysterious and strange, and I want to know how," I answered.

"Well, don't let curiosity overwhelm you. There's no reason to endanger yourself by getting entangled with that house," my mother snapped. "Eat your dinner and go to bed."

I did what I was told. I always did. But no matter what my mother enforced, I didn't keep my eyes off that house. There was something off about it, something utterly peculiar. That house and its owners were a suspect, and I was going to crack the mystery behind them.

***

My alarm beeped ding, ding, ding. I tumbled out of bed, yawning, but trotted downstairs. Then, being the quietest little mouse I could be, I crept out of the house into the fresh, morning air. A boy, rubbing his eyes, approached my way. "Nora, it's so early. Do we have to go today?"

"This is the only time we have to investigate Logan. Now let's go."

Crossing the street, Logan tagged along until we reached our suspect. The creepy house.

Why was the house a suspect? Why was I so "entangled" with it? Well, that could be explained the first week we moved here. My mother's gazes at that particular family portrait of us, including my dad, might've been the reason she ignores the house, but it shouldn't be ignored.

***

Every morning, after my mom makes me breakfast, I grab my supplies for school and head outside. "Now, Nora, I want you to go straight to school and back home," she always said. I always nodded, understanding what she meant. Then, her gaze would always turn to a photo with my father in it. And we would be silent, trying to push the tears in.

Oh, how I missed my father. How I always longed for him, and recalled how he was taken from me. The house across from ours had been there for a long time, even before we moved here. A few days after we had settled in, there was a bunch of racket coming from there while we were trying to sleep. So, my father knocked on their front door. We had never seen or heard from whoever lived inside.

After a series of knocks, we heard a scream and to our dismay, my father had disappeared. We informed the police, but their investigation led to nowhere. They were unable to enter the house, having lock-picked it and attempted to destroy it. And, the invisible evidence from outside didn't tell us anything of my father's disappearance either. Frightened, they closed the investigation. As a result, my father's still missing. It's been a little more than a month.

Following this investigation, people began to cower in Nacogdoches, the town that we live in. The fact that this house was impenetrable really frightened them. So, precautions were set around everywhere, therefore limiting any curious opportunities.

I might've not known what the house's owners' intentions were with their faces hidden, but I knew what mine were: find my father, crack the mystery of their creepy house, and send the monsters to jail. The police might've closed the investigation, but I reopened it, and I had help. To do this, I would wake up earlier than my mother – honestly, earlier than everybody – and meet Logan by that house. Together, we would investigate the house and search for clues. Logan fit this description as his father was a very successful detective, and I think I've watched enough crime movies.

***

Logan approached the front door as he dusted the door frame, searching for any fingerprints of my father's or his suspect. But like yesterday, there were no cracks or any fingerprints that could be used. Not even my father's. This was probably why the investigation was closed. After my father disappeared, two officers skimmed through clues involving the basic ones we were consulting but reported only of the mysterious complexity. Following the investigation, the police department didn't destroy the house; they just left it like it was in the beginning. As a result, it was never vanquished for the evil crimes the owners might've committed.

I squinted with one eye as I peeked through the hole in the wooden board. But, the curtains were pulled tight, so all I saw was the dark fabric. I guess it also didn't help that there wasn't much daylight.

With nothing else to investigate, I hurried back home just before my mother woke up. I had a breakfast of delicious strawberry pancakes right before I got my supplies and started for the door. "Nora, please come back home after the bus gets here." Her voice sounded direct but it was built on anxiety. I nodded before watching my mother turn to the photo of my father's, turning away myself. I held the tears in before I caught the bus and another problem. "Hey, Nora!" someone called out. I turned.

"Oh hi, Veronica," I tried my best to smile. The girl in front of me was Veronica, my frenemy, who always had to meddle in everything I did and stick her nosy mouth in my business. This worked in her favor as my parents had made sure that I became friends with her. She was our neighbor, the one that actually greeted us when we moved here. But they're not just going to force friends on me. I won't let them. To my luck, she hadn't found me by that house yet. Hopefully, she never would. So as the bus screeched to a stop, I hustled off, eager to lose Veronica. She definitely wasn't going to distract me from my dad.

***

After the bus stopped on my street after school and I had spent a difficult 15 minutes chatting with Veronica about her new Instagram post, I focused my attention on the suspect in front of me. All I could feel was fear, impatience, and anger towards this house and most importantly their mysterious owners. It was like fire in my eyes, and this creepy aura surrounding the house that I tried my best not to shake me down. I glared, I calmed, and then I stiffened. But as I stared at the house for what might be my dad or a hidden clue, I noticed something. The lawn. The grass was bright green, unlike ours despite our attempts at watering it. So, how was theirs green if no one ever came out to supply water? Unfortunately, I couldn't investigate right now.

But, the questions stuck in my mind the entire night while in bed. How was that possible? Did someone actually live there? Did they come out one time? How come no one has ever seen them?

I dropped my shoulders and jerked my body to face my boring white wall. My brain grew tired of thinking. All I wanted was an answer. All I wanted was my dad back at home, helping my mother carry on with our lives. All I wanted was Veronica out of my life, and Logan to help me figure out this complex mystery. Unfortunately, only one of my wants were being fulfilled.

As I laid in bed, unable to sleep, I transitioned to the clues but didn't get to anywhere useful. Even though the house seemed to lack stability and good conditions, there was no physical evidence anywhere. It's as if the person who lives there erased all the vulnerabilities.

I turned to face the clear sky through my window. The moon shone brightly in the night sky, forming a gibbous shape. But, despite the moon's brightness, something else was lighting up that caught my attention. The creepy house. After being dark all this time, the windows of the house lit up as the moon seemed to dim along with it. Seriously, the Moon wasn't bright anymore. It looked like a New Moon now.

I jerked out of bed and ran to my window. The house

was dark again, but the light had revealed a figure. A silhouette of a man or at least someone with short hair. So, someone actually lived there…

***

All I wanted now more than ever was to get inside that house and discover the man's physical qualities, so I could ruin his life or his accomplice's once and for all. But how was I going to do that? The house was "impenetrable," somehow invulnerable and was unable to be breached. The house might've lit up for a second, but now it was as dark as tar. Right now, I felt the burning stage of hopelessness.

However, I crawled back into bed, curious about this revelation with the Moon. How was it possible that it suddenly dimmed? Could it be a ghost or a spirit? Something that sucks on moonlight? Before I could think any further, the house gave an opening. A man had just left with the door wide open. He turned to the side and was too far away to make sight of his face, but I could see that he was a man.

At that moment, without thinking, my heart gave in and I did what I had been longing to do.

"Logan, you there?" I spoke softly through my walkie-talkie that I had convinced Logan to buy. "Psst, pssssst. Logan are you there?"

"Nora?" a voice answered with a yawn. "What's going

on?"

"I need your help, Logan. It's urgent. Meet me outside your house in five minutes or less."

"What?" Logan asked before I put down the walkie-talkie and quickly changed into more proper attire for outside.

***

"Are you kidding me? Are you frickin' crazy?!" Logan shrieked after hearing my plan. "We are not doing that! I have no interest in getting arrested for trespassing or getting killed! What if the owners are psycho?! We've never seen them!"

"Okay, well, first, keep it down, or we're actually going to get caught. And second, we're not gonna get arrested. We're just kids."

"We're teenagers, not kids. And juvie?"

I brushed off his ridiculous comments. "Look, that man left the door open. We can go in and find my father."

Logan sarcastically laughed. "Yeah, this faceless dude left the door open just so two kids can walk in and find a missing father." At his last words, I turned away and faced the ground, trying to resist the push of tears from my eyes.

Logan sighed. "Okay, look, I'm sorry, but this is ridiculous. That's not how criminals work. The suspect doesn't just leave the door open to where they keep their hostages. I think it's just a trap."

My brain comes to fight, but my heart leaps forward, winning. My father's absence is too unbearable to be compared with the absurdity of this open-ended plan or honestly no plan. So, that's exactly what I told Logan. "I haven't seen my father in so long, and I can't just continue grieving or living without him any more. We have been searching for clues for just a short period of time, but there isn't anything to be found. The inside of that house is the answer and we should take it."

Logan hesitated, and then said. "But, what if your father isn't around anymore?"

I quickly leaped at his question. "Don't worry about that."

He dropped the topic. "Okay, but I think it would be safer if we called the cops. Maybe they can get a warrant and no one gets in trouble."

"Ha ha, the same police who ran from the investigation? No, we are doing this ourselves. Forget about the stupid warrant. We are going in, and finding my father, and arresting the lunatic owners." As I said this, I just hoped these series of events would happen. While part of me was not skeptical, the other half was — well, one third was. But, I shook it off as I turned towards what would be the resolution of a happy ending.

I grabbed Logan's hand and pulled him forward. He sighed, but quit whining.

"Nora?" a voice spoke.

Oh no. Someone caught me. My mom is going to be furious.

I immediately stopped, giving a second to take in the minutes after this run-in when I would be in trouble. But, as soon as I turned, Veronica was staring at me, her eyebrows wrinkling. "What are you doing?"

"Uh… nothing," I replied. Finally I said, "It's none of your business, Veronica."

"You can't just sneak around in the middle of the night," she reasoned. "Does your mom know you're here?"

"It's none of your business. Come on, Logan." I turned away from her.

"What are you two up to?"

I locked my eyes on the wide, open door of the house in front of me, pulled Logan, and ran away from Veronica's whines. "Wait, that godforsaken house is forbidden," she called.

"It's not forbidden, just forgotten on purpose. Unlike the police, I'm going to solve the mystery behind it."

"I'm coming with you."

"There's no need for that, Veronica," Logan answered, turning.

"You can't stop me," she replied.

I took a heavy groan with a subtle eye roll. I hit my forehead with my palm before answering, "Fine, just come with us, then."

Without wanting to hear Logan or Veronica's reactions,

I crossed the valley of grass and approached the door of the house. I stuck my hand through the doorway, then motioned for Logan and Veronica to join me. "Wait, we're going inside?!" Veronica shrieked.

"Keep it down, or someone is going to catch us," I said.

As soon as we had entered the house, the door abruptly closed behind us. Veronica ran to the door and tugged on it the hardest she could, but it remained locked. I took a short glance at the conundrum.

"How will we go back home?" she whimpered, right before I pulled her and Logan away from the door. I would figure out the door thing later.

"This is why I told you not to come."

"But Nora, how will we go back? I told you this was a bad idea," Logan whispered to me.

I shook my head, ignoring their comments. I turned on my flashlight and shined it across the interior of the house, but something seemed off as the light came on. The flashlight wasn't shining on all of the darkness. As we continued to walk deeper into the house, the flashlight only lit up half of the dark, and the dark never stopped. "Why does the inside look larger than the outside? And why are none of the lights turned on?" Logan asked.

Suddenly, I was burdened by a bad feeling. Oh, stupid heart. I should've used my head.

"Are you sure about this, Nora?" both my proteges

asked. Only now, I wasn't so sure anymore. This black pool of darkness overwhelmed me, and every bit of confidence I had locked up inside was escaping. To be honest, I was terrified. Now, I just wanted my mother. But, thinking back to the lonely tears of her eyes, I reminded myself that I have to get my father back. Not to just appease her tears, but to appease the sadness and loneliness I have bottled inside for the last month.

Finally, I found a traditional part of a house. A staircase. Where as everything else seemed peculiar, the staircase looked absolutely normal. I approached it, staring at the dim upstairs with a hopeful look on my face. Even though the whole house was shrouded in darkness, I knew there was light up there. I was also wishing that there would be light up there. How does the owner even live here in complete dark?

But, as I approached the stairs, I heard a sound of a person. It was ringing in my ears. I pinched my temples to avoid the ugly and hate-filled voice as it spoke and spoke in small abrupt sentences. "Hello? Can you hear me?" it said. I tried shaking my head to get rid of the creepy tone. "Can I help you… what are you doing in my home… Nora… hello… it's time for you… like your father…"

I screamed. I covered my head to get rid of the voice, but I started seeing visions of an "x". Then a mirror. Then an x on a mirror. I continued to scream. I was feeling faint. I rocked my head back and forth as my friends hustled to console me. They murmured sounds of confusion and comfort, but I wasn't paying attention to them. My head was aching, and my ears were hurting. The visions didn't stop. The sound didn't stop. And worse of all, this feeling didn't stop.

But then — just a millisecond later — there was an end, a state of finality to the craziness I was imagining. Was I actually going crazy? No, I couldn't possibly be. I took my hands off of my face and over my head, and my eyes looked forward. I was in a room. My friends were nowhere to be found. And, when I turned…

***

Nothing made sense. The X on the mirror started to talk. It was the one from my vision, perched innocently in the middle of the attic. I was appalled by the voice. It was the same creepy tone I had heard downstairs. And now, it was attached to some entity. Wait, no, that can't be right. Supernatural creatures aren't real. I'm just imagining everything. There's no face in the mirror. There is no mirror. It's just my imagination. It's just my imagination. It's just my imagination…

No, it's not my imagination. There actually was an entity in the mirror. It spoke to me, "Nora, I guess it's time for you now."

I was already shaken by this supernatural being. When I heard my name, I was completely speechless. Was I the main character of some movie who the villain already knew of? At this minute, that's exactly what it felt like. So, being completely confused with this plot right here, I said the first word that came to my mind — the first word that would describe this whole situation. "Umm, what?"

I could tell that was not the response the entity was looking for. So, I asked a follow-up question. "What are you? How are you in the mirror? How do you know my name?"

"Right, humans don't really believe in supernatural creatures. Here's the deal: I'm trapped here for all eternity, but you can change that."

"Excuse me?"

"Yes, and if you don't, your father will die."

"My father? You have him?" My heart skipped a beat and my mind started to race with doubt and longing.

"Yes, I have him. He was very stupid, knocking on my door."

Suddenly, my confused state turned to anger. How dare this strange, weirdo entity talk about my father like that. "He was trying to keep you quiet, you filthy x, whatever you are. We were trying to sleep." My eyebrows lowered and I almost squinted.

"I am actually a Destroyer. And I will kill him if you don't cooperate."

"Okay, look, Destroyer, whatever you are, I have absolutely no idea why you need me, but I'm here for my father."

"Yes, your father. I said that I will return him if you help me."

The word "father" hit me, but I replied with what any typical person would say that their parents have taught them. "I'm not helping a stranger. I don't know anything about you."

The Destroyer took a pause and then answered, "Okay, I will tell you about my origins. My family comes from a line of the Destroyers: the people who are destined to create chaos on this Earth. Very cringy it might sound, but we took pleasure in it all because of the Creators. The Creators of the World from long ago shunned our family. We never used to be evil, but they saw something dark in our hearts, so that's exactly what we became. And, obviously the Creators had to meddle with our business and prevent the Apocalypse, so they created the line of the Saviors to imprison the Destroyers." He abruptly stopped speaking. *What the heck is this dude saying?*

Affected by his sudden pause, I motioned him to continue. If I was being forced to help this Destroyer X thing, then he had an obligation to give me all the details. And now, as I listened to all this rubbish, I was seriously contemplating to leave this room and find my father and leave this stupid house with everyone safe in their homes. But, I needed a distraction. Villains in movies love to chat evil and that's their weakness.

"And?" I asked.

"What do you mean 'and?' Why do you think I need you? You're the next Savior. The doppelganger of the woman who put me inside this prison." His words hit me in the head. Me, a Savior? I was a descendant of the mythical Saviors, destined to imprison these Destroyers? Yeah, I think not.

All I could do was laugh. "No, I'm sorry, I'm not a Savior. And you're not a Destroyer. I'm just imagining everything or dreaming." And with all of this hysterical rubbish too unbearable, I turned and leapt for the open door behind me, something I should've done before all this nonsense came about. However, as I hurried towards the door, it closed automatically — all by itself. Now, I was truly speechless. Is magic real? Is what this thing saying true? I turned around as the X in the mirror answered everything. "What I'm saying is true. Magic is real. And that was the work of my little helper."

"Helper?" My lips quivered and a shiver went down my body. I guess I never thought that this entity wouldn't be alone.

"Yes, my helper. The man who left the door open for you today, and the man who you saw this night as the house lit up." *So this was really all a trap. Everything was planned.* "He's the one who enchants the house, makes it unable to be trespassed, gives it the creepy look, hides any clues, and etc." *So that's where the invincibility comes from.*

"What is the X for?" I asked.

"It marks the place where I reside, temporarily. The Saviors marked all of their prisons to distinguish them from other mirrors. So, I guess you could say, X marks me, the suspect of your investigation."

He began to laugh creepily, or maybe it was in my head. But, I couldn't take it anymore. This whole situation was getting to me. I screamed for help. "Logan! Veronica!"

"Sorry, my helper took care of them. The only way to release them, including your pathetic father is to help me. Get rid of this X that marks my spot, and release me from this horrid prison.

"How?" I cried.

Suddenly, I could see visions in my head again. The way to get rid of the x. The house, the mirror, the man, and me. I would have to get rid of me. I would have to be trapped in the mirror for eternity. I would have to take this Destroyer's place.

I reviewed the whole situation. As a Savior, I knew I shouldn't even be fidgeting with the decision to let the X and the Destroyer go. But, I my father whooshed through my mind. He was innocent and my mom has been crying and crying over his absence as well as I. I would never see him again, but she would. And, anyways, who needs a disobedient and absent daughter when you can have a loving husband? A few tears streamed down my face at these thoughts. My lip quivered again. Maybe I wasn't that confident anymore.

Then there are Veronica and Logan. I don't care about Veronica, but both of them stood by me as I struggled this last month and explored the house. Well, Veronica whined, but she was there.

"Fine, I'll help you. But you have to swear that you will

release my father and my friends."

"Yes, of course."

"And, you have to promise you won't cause mayhem on this Earth." My lip stopped quivering.

The Destroyer was hesitant to answer. "I'm sorry, but my duty on this Earth is to cause the Apocalypse to hurt the Creators. You can choose: save your father or save the Earth."

"No, you will not bring the Apocalypse. I was months without my father; I think I can survive more. And, if you kill him, I will never help you." My voice was stern and direct. I was done being afraid of this trapped entity.

The Destroyer, filled with anger, spoke, "Very well. I will try to mend my ways for freedom, but I make no promises."

"One last question," I abruptly spoke.

The Destroyer, annoyed and exasperated said, "What?" It almost sounded like his voice rattled the walls of this century old house.

"Do the Saviors come from my mom's side or my dad's?"

"Your mom's. I doubt I would kidnap someone of Savior descent. And anyways, the Creators believed in more female power than male. They figured that females were less corruptible than males. It's complete nonsense. And before you ask, she's not a Savior." The exasperation and annoyance in his voice increased, and I could tell our deal might be off if I didn't stop.

I simply nodded. And, as guilty as I felt, I stood back and put a hand out to absorb the Destroyer's aura and soul. He slowly exited the X and it disappeared. In a matter of seconds, his soul was being subsumed by a body. He rose above me, taller than I expected, and smiled. I could see a white reflection in his eyes. I had no idea where it was coming from.

He replied with a thank you and looked at me before I completed the final step. As I took one last final look at him, I couldn't help but look into his white eyes, tears flowing down mine.

But looking back at the mirror, I subtly wiped my tear. I swallowed my spit. And I took a deep breath. I moved my hand down in a diagonal motion, forming an X on the mirror, and with one look outside the window nearby, I propelled myself into the darkest depths of the lonely mirror. I could feel my body clash with the surface of the mirror before feeling the nothingness of air inside the small dark space. The Destroyer left the room without so much as a glance towards me while all I could do was stare from the prison surrounding me; the dark clouds of the world inside the mirror fogging my eyes and taking over my body.

***

The sun peeked through the curtains and into my room, shining all over my bed. It hit my eyes, and even with my eyes closed, I could see this orange light. I slowly opened my eyes, and there was the sun, shining as brightly as it could on the side of my pulled curtains. Hmm, it had been awhile since the sun had shone. Actually, no, it was sunny yesterday. Wait, no, it was cloudy yesterday. It was always cloudy through the mirror; before that, it was always cloudy without my father.

I'm confused. I remember yesterday to be cloudy, but I also remember there to be sun. And wasn't I trapped in the mirror? How have I awoken in my bed on the sunniest day possible? This must all be a dream — a very happy dream. There is no other explanation. But why does everything feel so real?

I gave myself a pinch, and I felt it. Good and strong. This is real life. Wait a minute, where's my father? Didn't I release him? And how about Logan and Veronica? Through all this X-mirror and father episode, I completely forgot about them.

As I wrapped my head around this happy environment surrounding me, the door to my room opened and my mother stepped in. "Oh, good morning, sweety. Good, you woke up."

I stared at her, finding a happy glare in her eyes, trying to find any sense of an explanation. But she caught on. "Nora, are you okay?"

I was quick to answer. "Yes, I'm fine. Mom, are you okay?"

She lowered her eyebrows with a puzzled expression on her face. "Yes, dear, I'm quite alright." *So, my dad must be home.*

My mom soon left my room as I brushed my teeth, constantly staring at myself in the mirror. *The mirror, the mirror, the mirror...*

I had lonely moments in there — dark moments. How was I able to escape it all? Even a good dream seems preposterous. The prison was meant to make the Destroyers suffer, similar to how it had been crippling me for countless days.

When I went downstairs, I couldn't help but ask my mother, "Is Dad home?"

She couldn't help but smile. "You know, just because you have summer break doesn't mean he does. He's at work."

"At work?" I repeated. I was left speechless. My father, he, he, he, was back. I got him back. I *did* it.

That whole day was filled with the longing for my father. I couldn't wait until he would cross the threshold of my front door and give me a hug. My focus was nowhere else. In fact, I stopped thinking about Logan and Veronica. Although that might've been selfish of me, my mother told me that we were having a dinner party that evening. So, I would be able to talk with the two people who could provide me an explanation to all this craziness I was facing.

***

My father had finally arrived.

As I peeked through the window, he made his way up the front steps right as he rang the doorbell, and I, as tingly as ever, opened the door for him and ran to his arms, embracing him fully.

I could tell he was shocked, but I didn't care. All that mattered was that he was home, here in my arms. "Hi, Nora. Wow, you are happy today. What's going on?"

I opened my mouth to speak, but I couldn't form the words. I was staring at my father's face. I hadn't seen him for months. But there he was, his warm smile and large eyes staring back at me. However, finally, I answered, "Nothing. I'm just excited that you're home and I get to spend time with Veronica and Logan today."

"Glad to hear it. But, who's Logan and who's Veronica? Are these some new friends I don't know about?"

My eyes quit blinking and stared straight at my dad's face. What did he just say? "Uh, they're my friends," I told him, stammering at his weird question.

"Oh, did you invite them over today?" His eyes were kind and the few aging lines on his face only reminded me of the warm father I had before. But, I couldn't move past his question. Something was wrong. I must be having another dream. I must be in some other reality. I must be still in the mirror. I must be, I must be, I must be...

***

Only, I was not. I wasn't having a dream, I wasn't in some other reality, and I wasn't stuck in the mirror. The whole day felt real.

I was shook by how Logan and Veronica's name didn't ring a bell to any of my parents. But, after staring at their puzzled expressions, I came up with the idea to tell them that they were some new kids at my school; suspicion and confusion soon wiped off their face. But, it surely didn't leave mine. How could the one person who my parents had been forcing me to befriend just leave their minds? And how could the one true friend who they knew so much about not exist anymore? I don't understand how Veronica turned from being my neighbor to not existing; the same went for Logan. Had I imagined them? Had I been dreaming them? Honestly, I wasn't so sure of anything anymore.

However, even if nobody knew of Veronica and Logan, everything felt real and happy. Happy. Wait, life can't be happy. No, it can't be. My life hasn't been happy for a long time. This must be a dream. This must be the mirror playing tricks on me. But this was a hard thought to be able to fathom and digest, especially with the true happiness and joy I was feeling right then and there.

That evening, guests came over for dinner. I was

guessing that they were all our *real* neighbors, but to be honest, I didn't recognize most of them, especially the two strangers my age who came and hugged me. They took me by surprise, and their sudden gossip caused even more confusion. If there's one thing about me, it's how much I despise gossip. Especially gossip about social trends and what not.

Throughout the whole evening, I peeked at their phones and found out that their names were Anna and McKenna. They were twins who were apparently my best friends and whom I had texted a bunch of memes, gifs, cliches, messages, and TikToks. Weird, I don't remember doing any of this. But the strangest part of the evening was the eerie people who called themselves our neighbors. From across the street. The neighbors that owned the "suspect" house. The people who were faceless.

Apparently, they were not. As they sauntered into my house, my parents introduced me to them, claiming that they had just moved here. The couple shook my hand and told me that their names were Mr. and Mrs. Ex. X. *The X. The Destroyer.* Those were the first words that ringed through the mind. However, before I could display the sudden memory of those horrid events, the couple told me that their last names were a little unusual, being spelled as "E-x" versus "X" as many people thought. But, the X was all that I was reminded of. That horrid X. Why did this person have to remind me of that great big X and that great big monster I had unleashed?

I stared up at the man's face and as I did, there was something familiar about his eyes with a clean, white reflection. And now, as I stared at him, there was something familiar about his height. He was tall, and had dark hair. And, suddenly, I knew exactly how.

***

As the guests were starting to leave, I casually slipped out of the house. The night can't end before I do this. And, this was the only opportunity I had to explain all this craziness.

As our neighbors, Mr. and Mrs. Ex, started for their home, I trailed them, hiding behind a large tree on their yellowish grass. Before, it used to be bright green, almost as if a very dedicated gardener came out and took care of the grass. Now, it was just like any regular lawn. As the couple unlocked their door, they hurried inside, but to my surprise, they left it open. When they got farther away from the door, I, being the quietest little mouse I could – again – walked inside the house with luck on my side. As soon as I stepped in, the house gave a bright glow. Most of the lights were turned on, and the inside was the size of ours. Not bizarrely huge or covered in a pool of darkness.

I crawled up the stairs until I came to the staircase leading to the attic. Shifting back and forth between aborting and going up, I eventually chose tiptoeing up the stairs. As I hurried up the steps, the dim lights lit my way up until the point where there were no more lights. Just darkness and the moon sending a bit of light through a window. Well, actually no, there is supposed to be a New Moon today. Very surreal.

Pretty soon, I arrived in the attic. Their attic was tiny like ours, and something caught my eye right as I stepped in. A mirror. It was the mirror from before. The mirror which caged the Destroyer. It had the huge, red "X" on it. I approached it, and from a few moments of staring at an ordinary mirror, fog partially clouded the surface; what I saw after the fog disappeared was too unbelievable to fathom.

Through the dark and silvery surface of the mirror, the vague sights of a girl with the same face as me stared back at me, her eyes a dark color from the torture of the mirror. And, in the background, the sudden sound of footsteps left me feeling cloudy in my mind. I stepped to the side, hiding behind a large box, staring at the ground and trying to make sense of what I had just seen.

Mr. Ex stepped into the attic, staring at the mirror. And suddenly, I realized, X didn't mark the Suspect or the Destroyer. Instead, X marked the Savior. And it has for a while.

Just Fly

Prologue

"Quick, swarm the food before they come back!" my mother buzzed as a I circled a plate of food in midair.

With her eyes set on her goal, she descended onto the border of the plate with me and my father trailing behind. As we landed, our hypopharynx (tongue-like tubes) extended and began sucking on the delicious treat that the humans had left behind. I felt a tangy, sweet flavor travel down to my stomach as the food was liquefied. My and my parents' wings flapped with joy as every single micrometer was scraped off with our exhilarated hypopharynx. In our enjoyment, we avoided making buzzing noises with our wings, but it was easier said than one.

Our uninterrupted enjoyment was cut short. Before we

could finish the delicious treat, the humans rushed from deep inside the house, swatting at us ferociously. The male grabbed a stick with a flat end and began whacking it on the table. We slightly swayed from one side to another in response. But, my parents smirked wickedly at me, and before the humans could squish our tiny bodies, they swerved and dodged the stick. I performed a back flip to avoid the stick and accompanied my parents as they flew out an ajar door.

Once we were outside, we felt the immediate rush of the air pulling against our wings. And, with a sharp turn, we faced the dumb-founded humans and laughed at their incompetent attacks. My father turned to me and said, "Amazing job, Volare. That was some mighty flying."

"Thanks, dad," I beamed at him, staring at the large sun in the distance and the huge outline of the humans inside the house. In fact, it seemed that the house itself and the bright blue sky was smiling right back at me, the sun being the eye and the house's large rooftop being the smile.

You might be wondering: what am I? I certainly can't be a human, and I'm not. I'm a fly. And this is the life of a fly. Well, it is my wondrous life. I loved flying with my small family through human houses, dodging the huge creatures for a bite of their tasty food stashed away on counter tops; then, soaring through the wide open sky where the birds were out of our reach. Some flies might've been scared to even dare to approach the humans and sail the skies, but my family was the exact opposite. We longed for danger and adventure. Life would be dull otherwise.

My mother started to speak. "I have to say, that was a delicious lunch. Let's go see if we can find dessert." With the three of us all smiling, we flew up higher into the air, gaining sight of most of the neighborhood with our tiny eyes.

Like my father had stated before, my name is Volare which meant "soar" in our language. According to my parents, that name suited me. It was evident that I was a really good flier – just like a bird could be. In fact, when I cracked open my pupa, I naturally had the nerve to flap my wings and soar into the beautiful blue sky. Once I started, I could immediately escape the grasp of humans and predators in general. It was like the feat of flying was woven into me. And this helped with the passion for human food. Oh, those humans. They're food has such a beauty to it, but they can never learn to share. We flies don't have that many food options, but they seem to have plenty. However, instead of sharing, they swat us when we try to suck on their food that they themselves wasted. Don't they know sharing is caring?

But, no matter how threatening the humans seemed, my family never once feared them. Instead, we turned it into a game, trying to tease the humans as they chased us through their home. In addition, my parents weren't scared of me ever getting squished by the hands of humans, nor the predators that attacked us. They knew how fast and agile I was. Well, I always thought they believed that.

My parents were always fearless and brave with nothing on their mind except fun, but after an incident with the humans — resulting in two deaths — they lost their bravery and sense of adventure. They stopped going in and out of human houses to eat the lovely food the humans possessed. They stopped feeling the longing to want to travel into the sky and beyond, and they lost any will to steal human food. In fact, change was influenced in my colony by them all because of the incident.

While my colony used to split up into families to search for food in different locations, we all swarmed together and sought refuge in a hollow tree from the vile humans and the ferocious birds. We each claimed a section in the tree, and stayed there. Volunteers to scavenge food were the only flies who were allowed to leave, and they were forbidden to find food in the human houses. To help maintain this system, we created a pact, and every fly signed it out of fear.

I was just a young fly at that time; now, I've completely grown, but my passions and motivations remain the same. This heart is longing for more than a hollow, enclosed tree can offer. These wings need more flying than the low ceilings of this tree. And, my stomach needs the satisfying sensation of human food.

Chapter 1

I darted through the dark hallways in the tree and found my room through the variety of open rooms in the tree.

Hurrying through the doorway, I stared out at the view of the pretty neighborhood from the large hole in my room. The dark green trees swayed in the distance. The Sun hid behind the row of houses, and through it all, the existence of nature and the ugly humans are what made it beautiful. Well, maybe the humans aren't ugly, and maybe their existence isn't really beautiful. Their food, on the other hand, is.

I've stared out of this hole ever since we made a pact to never leave the tree unless for scavenging or emergency purposes. I guess I was lucky to end up with such a pretty sight. But as I stared at the row of houses and the trees swaying in the wind, the memory came back to that day — the day when my happy, perfect life turned upside down.

My aunt and uncle were traveling with us, rushing ahead to beat us to a human's house they had located. They zoomed in through the doorway just as it was closing, leaving us stranded outside. I sighed, really wanting to taste the tasty food that lay inside. However, my parents waited patiently as they searched for a crack or opening to the house. However, there were none. For the first time ever, the incompetent humans did a good job leaving zero cracks.

I stared at the inside through a window at my aunt and uncle to see what food they would find. There were a few bowls of some creamy leftovers on the table. I stared enviously at the sight. Leftovers were the best, especially the creamy ones.

My aunt and uncle locked eyes on the marvelous sight. However, before they could approach the food, they started shaking. Their wings began shutting close. Their whole body tilted as I could see that they began to lose consciousness. Then, they dropped to the floor. My parents came in from behind, pulling me as I tried to resist, and flapped their wings hard to get away from the window. But, all I could do was just stare at the sight. Just stare and stare. I don't remember if a tear came out, but I was definitely left completely confused and dismayed. I fumbled as my parents pulled me away, and several thoughts and questions went through my mind. *Why were they taking me away? What happened to them in the house? How could my parents just leave them there, unconscious?! We had to save them!*

When my parents got a good mile away from the house, they stopped, catching their breath. I stopped almost lifeless — shocked and speechless. Finally, I opened my mouth as they tried to look innocent. "Why would you just leave them behind?! They're unconscious, we have to save them!" I started to turn.

"I'm sorry, Volare, but we have to get away from there," my mother told me, concern in her voice. She stared down at the far ground below, trying not to look me in the eye. This was the first time I had seen her like this. No stability, just worry.

"Why?!" I demanded.

My parents turned to each other before finding the correct words. "Your aunt and uncle aren't unconscious. They're dead."

I automatically flinched, flying a step back. The words stung me in the ear. "What do you mean they're dead?" I stared at their worried eyes, worry flooding into mine. They turned back to each other, but I needed an answer. "What happened, mom, dad? Why are they dead? How did they die?"

She didn't answer. Instead, my father did. "Insecticide," he answered. He said with such animosity and also fright.

They stood in silence for a few minutes. All I could do was ask the obvious. "What is insecticide?" I asked.

"I've heard about it from other flies, but I never took it

seriously," my father said. "It's an invisible method to kill flies."

"Invisible? They're that developed?" I asked. I couldn't believe it. Humans, the struggling fly whackers, had found new ways to get rid of us. They were so bad at attacking us tiny insects that they decided to let something else do the work for them.

"But it is only this one house," I stated, remaining hopeful. "I'm pretty sure that that most houses don't have insecticide," I told them, trying to feel optimistic with each word. I think I could feel a tear almost forming.

"It's invisible, Volare. We don't know which houses will have insecticide," my mother stated, igniting my true fears. With great meaning in her voice, she said, "I always knew that humans were trouble. I can't believe I just ignored all this danger. And I put you in jeopardy." She looked at me.

"I'm fine, mom. Really. And, I always thought you didn't fear humans."

"Humans are everything to fear. They're so much larger than us. So much stronger than us. If they had access to such a variety of foods, I'm pretty sure they could think of other ways to kill flies," my mother said.

Wait, what? No, this can't be true. I started to stammer. "But, but, but, adventure, risk, fun." My parents were neglecting my words.

"Your mother's right," my father said. I couldn't

believe it. My father was a fly of passion, exploit and risks. He was the fiercest one I knew after my mother. Fear never affected him; fear of humans definitely wasn't even a term for him. And all because of something that happened in *one* house.

"But, but," I started to argue again. "Flies live all over human houses. We live all over human houses."

"We can find a home out here. Maybe in a tree large enough for the whole colony."

"But we travel in families, not together as a whole. And what is this about finding *a* home? We have multiple homes. We're nomads. All flies are nomads." I took a deep breath, staring fervently into their eyes. Could they not see the pain in mine?

My mother sighed. "Listen, many members of our colony are being killed: insecticide and predators. So, maybe it's just best just to keep everyone safe."

"But flies have short lives."

"Why make them shorter?" my mother asked which I knew was a statement. I started to open my mouth to argue, but for the first time ever, my mouth was truly in shock. My parents had broken my heart. They no longer seemed to be the heroes of my life.

This incident brought two deaths, but it felt like I had died myself. My own heart had dimmed and fallen at the place where my aunt and uncle both died. But, I brought it back to life because I need it when I escape this tree to my salvation.

***

As I looked out at the glorious sight, that last quote from my mother still clouded my memory. *Why make it shorter?*

That might've been true. But what was the use if you had to spend your life just cooped up in a tree without taking any risks? Life should not be about safety, but about action and uncertainty. What is living if it's just boredom the entire time? Every second of life should not be lived but enjoyed. And death comes after you have had all your fun. For me, that's probably not too far away — all the more reason to enjoy life now.

So, while my parents had forbidden me to leave this tree unless for scavenging — they never let me scavenge — I still found ways to escape this confinement, so I might try the tasty human foods again. All we get here is bitter organic matter. *Bleh!*

I turned my head to view the action going on in the hallway. It seemed pretty quiet and lifeless. Now was the time that I could escape.

Before flapping my wings, I turned around to mourn the tree, wondering if I would ever be wiling to come back here to this boring prison. Nope, I'm not sad at all.

I turned back around and started flapping my wings as I gently took off from the surface of the tree. I drifted out of the hole in my room and slowly made my way out from the shadow of the tree.

Finally, I escaped the tree's shadow and felt sunlight pouring all over me, my wings feeling the breeze. Yes, the angels in the clouds were definitely singing as I took to the air. And the bright blue sky was smiling once again. So, I started to flap my wings harder, and take off.

"Wow, you got farther than last time," a voice from behind me spoke.

My wings stopped, and I abruptly turned to face my mother staring at me back in the tree. I sighed to myself, and my wings flapped in disappointment as I entered the tree where she was waiting patiently.

"Now, you know the rules," she said for the billionth time when I stepped onto the bark.

"Yes, don't have fun and don't take risks," I replied, stating the truth.

She gave me a stern look.

I sighed again. "Don't leave the tree," I replied.

"Unless," she answered, "you get permission from an adult to scavenge for food."

"I am an adult," I told her. "And you never let me scavenge when I volunteer.

"That you are. But..." she paused. "You know why," she then said. "It's just to keep you safe. When you're ready to handle it, you will be sent. And about the fun: you can have plenty of fun in here."

I rolled my large, green eyes at her. I think it was pretty

obvious. Then I spoke, "We're flies. It's hard for us to be safe. Anything can squish us or hurt us. So why can't we just leave this tree and soar in the skies and have fun?"

"Like you said, we're flies, not birds," my mother stated.

"But the word fly is in our name," I stated.

"So? It's spelled "f-l-i" not "f-l-y."

"But, we used to soar in the skies."

"No, we didn't soar. We simply searched for food. And even if we did, predators were always tailing us. Isn't it better to be safe by not taking the skies?"

I felt sick listening to my mother's words. My stomach containing the bitter organic matter just wanted to gag. I decided to take my argument in a different direction. "Then, why did you name me Volare? Doesn't that mean 'soar?'"

"It does. But a name doesn't dictate how someone acts."

"But just because one house had insecticide doesn't mean all of them do."

"We can't take the chance," my mother warned. "Remember, it's invisible."

I tensed up. "Yeah, I know that. I just wish I could taste the human foods again." And, with my longing and desire revealed, I really hoped that it would change my mother's mind.

"Sorry, Volare, you are not leaving this tree." With that

said, my mother levitated out of my room. Levitate, that's all you could do in this stupid tree. You couldn't actually fly like you could outside. Everything was too narrow. We had turned into penguins. All they could do was levitate near the water.

I sighed as I looked up at the sight one last time, exiting my room into the empty hallway. My mother waited for me as I followed her into the large radial room where all the flies had gathered to socialize. *Socialize,* I laughed. Who's ever heard of a more ridiculous thing? That's what the bees do, not us.

My parents started to greet other flies, and even introduced me to some male flies. I forced my small mouth to smile, but it quickly vanished. They think they're so clever. However, the last thing I would be doing is mating with someone to have maggots. They fell in love and mated, and that's how it would go down with me. And my definition of a perfect male fly would be someone who could take me across the neighborhood to try the human foods once last time. Just one last time. After that, I would be inclined to just stay locked up in the tree.

Luckily, after all my awkward smiles, I found a small empty room in the back that was without a fly and parent-free. It was a more of a small corner, but I was grateful. I turned my head cautiously to make sure that no one was following me.

I spotted someone near the bark wall staring at me. But he turned away as I gazed at him, acting like he was innocent.

Either way, this was my time to escape. I leapt for the

room, away from the ridiculous term that is socializing.

When I approached the hole in the wall, I could get a side view of the neighborhood. Many houses had open windows or the backyard door left open. I extended my antennae, receiving delicious smells that made my mouth water. By the way, I have a strong sense of smell. Not to brag, but it's true.

I started to flap my wings slowly, careful not to make a ruckus. Wings could sometimes buzz if you flapped them too hard. Luckily, my wings cooperated and kept the silence I needed. I slowly started to ascend off the bark floor as my wings carried me through the hole made in the wall. However, I had not thought this through. I soon realized the hole was too tiny and couldn't fit my body. Whichever fly carved this hole made it especially for me to stay inside.

I tried flying backwards, but my thorax had gotten stuck in the hole. I shifted and pulled, but I couldn't fly free of the wicked hole's grasp.

To make it all worse, I noticed my wings had wrinkled a little. It felt like they were laughing back at me in this twisted situation. I really just wanted to glare and hit my useless wings. But then, I thought, no, my wings are what have allowed me to do what I do best. *Just relax*, I told myself. I will figure something out.

Just then, something dripped onto my abdomen. I turned around suspiciously, wondering if a fly had caught me and was drooling. Nope, no one was there. Just my abdomen.

And something slimy on it.

Then, something dripped again — this time near my thorax. I carefully extended my hand to touch it. It was sap. Sticky, slimy tree sap. Great job, tree, way to keep me stuck to you!

More sap fell from the ceiling. *Drip, drip, drip* onto my foreleg. And the extra sap made my current situation worse! Now, there was no hope for me to escape. I'd probably be stuck in this hole till the day I die, or possibly until my parents would find me and I'd get in trouble — an amazing way to make me agitated.

I took a deep breath, sighing to myself and my ridiculous escape attempt, only to realize how I was starving. Before thinking otherwise, I extended my hypopharynx and began to suck on the sap. Blah! It tasted so bland; it was nothing compared to the "syrup" I have tasted on those delicious circle-like things in human houses.

But, I forcefully got rid of the sap to quench my hunger and overcome this horrible predicament. Pretty soon, most of it was gone, and all that remained was my bulk of a body against the microscopic hole. I tried pulling harder and harder to see if I could break free.

Pull. Pull. Pull...
Stuck stuck stuck...
Pull. Pull. Pull...
Tug. Tug. Tug...

Release release release....Break free...

Finally, I broke free, feeling a tug near my abdomen. Nonetheless, I started to make my way out from the bark taking flight through the cool evening air. Aah, it was so refreshing. And, just before I got to enjoy the thrill of it all, I immediately stopped. All of a sudden, I started hurtling towards the ground.

I tried flapping my wings, but one of them ached when I tried. I turned to look at my thorax and found myself staring at a broken wing. Oh my flyness, no, my wing broke! What was I supposed to do now? I couldn't shout for help. My parents would find me and ground me. Like, actually put me in the ground, where the only food you could eat was the decayed matter the worms broke down.

I stared helplessly as the ground rushed towards my face. I closed my eyes as each millisecond went by. It wouldn't be long now. Wait. Just wait. Hold on a minute. I can't go down like this. Without thinking of the consequences, I screamed for help the loudest I could, "Help! Please help! My wing is broken!" Unfortunately, I had already escaped the shadow of the tree. Woo, go me.

As I continued to fall, I constantly thought about what my mother had said. *Why make your life shorter?* I should've listened to her. Right now, I was making my life shorter.

In just a few more seconds, it would be all over. I would arrive in the Underworld. I could see my life flash before my eyes, right as I touched the ground.

Chapter 2

Just a second later, I opened my eyes. I looked around and spotted the tree. The cruel tree. Of course the tree would be in the Underworld. I turned my head, and everything looked so bright. From what I had heard, the Underworld was dark.

I got up, but tripped on something, my legs aching. But, wait a minute. The afterlife shouldn't hurt. I glanced down, and realized I was caught in a net.

I flinched, shaking my head, constantly thinking about what had just happened. I looked back up to see if my parents had caught me or some human, but instead there was another fly. The one that was staring at me back in the tree. He flew towards me, holding the end of the net. "Are you okay?" he asked as he approached me.

"Yes, I am, thanks to you," I smiled at him, looking back down at the net and unable to fathom how I had gone from inevitable death to being alive.

"Well, I saw you sneaking out, so I figured you would get into trouble."

"Well, thanks for noticing. I was trying to go unseen, but I'm glad someone saw me." I could feel my heart slowly racing. I was so lucky that someone had actually noticed me.

He smiled back at me, and then asked, "By the way, what were you doing outside the tree. Normally, one doesn't leave the tree unless to find food. And, you don't look like the scavenger type."

"Well, I've tried scavenging, but nobody wants me to venture into human houses," I answered, starting to slowly calm down.

The fly looked confused. I looked down at his net. "Nice net. Handy."

He turned to his net. "Oh, thanks. I guess it's good to keep a net around." He looked up at me. "I don't think I've seen you before. What's your name?"

"I'm Volare."

"I've never heard of that name. I'm Frons."

"That's a cool sounding name. What does it mean?" I asked.

He immediately jumped at the question, "Uh nothing

too important. What does your name mean?"

"I like to think that it means soar, but I"m not really getting to do that."

"You know you're not a bird," he answered with a squint of his eye and a hint of obviousness or maybe judgment.

"I'm still a fly though, right. I don't live that long, so I might as well enjoy my life and fly like in the name."

He stared at me. "Wow, I've never met someone who thought like that," he remarked. I smiled, taking his response as a compliment.

Since I couldn't fly and my body was in pain, Frons held me back and slowly brought me back to the tree. It might seem weird: I trusting a stranger after staying with only my parents for so long. But, he seemed gentle and harmless. The only trait negative was how he thought like a regular fly. A boring, tedious fly.

Frons climbed in first, trying to pull me after. However, my broken wings tugged on my abdomen, causing me to get all unbalanced. Frons was forced to apply more strength and finally pulled me up. As I touched the ground of the tree, I heard buzzing. A fly was rushing towards us. Well, two were.

"Volare?!" my mother shouted. "Where were you?" To my horror, she spotted my broken wing. "What happened to your wing?" she shrieked.

I didn't answer.

My father came in from behind. "Volare?! What's

going on here?

I looked up at both of them, trying my best to ignore my mother's austere eyes; instead, I looked up at my father's stern, but forgiving eyes. "I'm sorry, I broke it." I slowly walked up to my father, leaning on him. "I was trying to escape, but the hole was too small, so my wing ripped."

My father sighed, looking down at me. Although I was avoiding my mother, I could picture her glare. My dad looked down at me. "You know now why we made the pact. The outside world is dangerous. Let's take you to the *flirmiary*." And, although I couldn't help but disagree with every single word he said, I kept my mouth shut and followed him to the flirmiary, continuing to avoid my mother's gaze. I seriously didn't need her eyes telling me how I was wrong to follow my dream.

The flirmiary was much like the human infirmaries we had visited before the incident but for flies. Ugh! I'll never go to those again. They have such disgusting food. Nothing like what you would find in a human house.

As I sat on the leaf bed, the *floctor* examined my wing. He gently started to apply some sap on it. I looked away, feeling the irony. Sap pretty much started this mess, but you needed it to fix it.

The floctor turned to look at my parents. "Her wing will be fine. There is a rip, but it should heal in a few weeks, and she should be up and flying in about a month or two."

Before my parents could react, I did. "A month?! That's way too long!" I cried, staring up at my parents.

"Now, it's not the floctor's fault you damaged your wing. He's trying to help," my mother told me.

"The best thing that you can do is rest and let it heal," my father said.

I stared up in shock. Rest? No, thank you. I'm not going to rest. My wings should be feeling the breeze, not lazing on some bed. These words coming out of my father's mouth was truly unbelievable. He used to soar like a bird. And now, somehow, he's lost all his confidence and will, but especially passion.

My parents and the floctor soon left the small room, leaving me stranded and helpless on this bed. It might have been comfortable, but I would never rest. I was a fly. My job was to fly.

"Sorry about your wing," a fly said, entering the room.

I looked up to see the fly who had saved me from my doom. "Oh, Frons." I sighed. "Thank you for saving me, but it doesn't look like anything good came from it."

His face was shocked. He was staring at me like I was crazy. I thought back to what I said and of course I managed to appear psycho. Then he asked, "What do you mean? You got to continue your life with your parents."

"I know, I know, I was exaggerating. Of course I'm thankful that I was saved and of course I love my parents, but there's this sense of rebellion with me when I don't get my way. Right now, I just want to fly free out of this tree that is caging me."

"You want to leave this tree that badly? I mean, it is protecting you." His tone brought along lots of disbelief.

I sighed. "Yeah, I do." I took a deep breath, suddenly realizing the lunacy of my words. "Because, I have a passion to fly and passions are what keep my life interesting." I took another sigh, staring out the hole near me which showed just a plain field.

Frons took a while before answering. "I'm sorry, passions? You have a passion to fly?"

I turned to him, now wondering if he was crazy. "Yes, my passion is to fly through the skies in and out of human houses like my family used to do before."

He stared at the ground before replying to me. "I've never heard of a passion like that. You're really determined aren't you?" I nodded in response. "Too bad your wing's broken," he said.

I sighed. "I know, it sucks. But every dream has obstacles." Both of us became silent as I grieved my situation. Suddenly, a thought occurred to me. I guess I can brag that I am a quick thinker, too."Wait, I can't fly, but you can."

Frons immediately looked up at me. "I'm sorry, what?" he asked. "What do you mean?"

I slowly got up, ignoring the pain of my broken wing.

"You can take me to the neighborhood and I can finally try the human food again."

Frons opened his mouth to say something but then closed it. He stared at me. "I'm sorry, Volare. I know you're determined to do this, but I'm not going to break a rule and get into trouble."

I stared as if saying, *So?*

However, Frons was ready to make an argument to change my mind. "Listen, Volare. We aren't birds who soar the sky. We're flies. We're tiny, fragile, and eat organic matter. We stay in a tree to protect ourselves, so we don't die. And we stay away from those human houses. Humans are larger than us and are more skilled. Don't you know of the invisible insecticide? I think it killed someone in our colony."

"Yeah, they were my aunt and uncle," I told him, avoiding his gaze.

"Oh, I'm sorry about that," Frons replied.

However, I tried to be enthusiastic. "Like you said, we're flies. So, let's fly. We can't keep shying away from the houses because of insecticide. We have to be brave and believe that we can do it. Either way, we have a short life. Let's make it count."

He looked up, staring at the lunatic in front of him. But, I was the only one there. I guess I said something crazy once again. "I don't want to make it shorter. And besides, the skies are filled with tons of birds that are migrating back here. Birds eat insects, you know." And suddenly, the phrase my mother told me rang through my mind. *Why make it shorter?*

"I can outrun a bird," I bragged. "I have before."

Frons didn't argue with my flying skills. Instead he replied, "Well, I'm not a good flier. I never have been. You might be stealthy and all, but I'm not. I haven't left the tree in so long and I never try to. Unlike you, my name hasn't given me any confidence to outrun birds. It just means brown. My parents liked the name so they gave it to me, and either way, the family trips into human houses weren't too memorable."

Frons needed my help; he needed guidance, and I was grateful to give it. With someone's name meaning brown, I guess it would tug on their confidence. I started to speak, "Listen, Frons. Just because I was named Volare doesn't mean I have the ability to escape birds or fly stealthily. That comes from here — I pointed to my heart — and a little bit from my wings, but mostly my heart. However, I am determined and confident in myself and although it might sound cringy, I definitely don't give up. I have this passion to keep flying and that is how I have become a good flier. Passion is what affects your motivations. If you find can "

I have to say: I think I did a good job with my pep talk. All he needed was to understand what passion is. Afterall, this intangible feeling cannot be shaken; it's what determines one's actions one's drives your life. Now, as I stared up at him, all I could wish for was that I had provided help to an uninspired fly. I had never met anybody who was so stubborn. Well, actually my mom. And, honestly, I didn't really mingle with anyone else. I despised socializing, and no flies were ever interested in talking about the human houses or sneaking past curfew to find food there. Don't worry, I never did that. Well, maybe I tried once.

However, despite my amazing pep talk, Frons still showed a sign of reluctance. Time to do things the hard way. I grabbed Frons and jumped out of the hole in the wall, feeling the cold breeze rub against my tattered wing as we hurtled towards the ground. "What are you doing?!" Frons shrieked.

"Helping you face your fear," I told him, zero concern in my voice. My life has flashed before; I think I can handle another moment like that.

But there was a lot of concern in Frons' green eyes. He immediately started flapping his wings, grabbing a hold of me and making his way to a branch on the tree. Then, he took a deep breath, and I think his heart probably stopped for a second.

"Volare?! Are you crazy? We could've died!" he shrieked again.

"No, we wouldn't because you would've flied us back into the tree."

"That's ridiculous! Didn't I tell you I was a bad flier?"

"If you were, how did you survive that large drop?"

"Fly adrenaline, Volare! How else?" he argued with

me. But, his face definitely changed.

He stared down at the bark ground, avoiding my gaze. I couldn't tell if he was thinking or simply just reliving the moment when his life flashed before his eyes. And, suddenly my guilt came full on strong. What was I thinking? I was so selfish. He probably didn't even trust me anymore, and he was the first fly I had met who had shown compassion to me. Why am I like this? I don't ever use my head.

I approached Frons. "Frons, I am so sorry. I don't know what I was thinking. We almost died, and your adrenaline saved us. I understand if you don't trust me anymore. I'm just too headstrong and too impatient."

Frons paused before answering. Then, he finally said. "No… it's fine," he said with a pause in between.

"No, it's not," I answered.

"Yes, it is," he said.

I smiled at his response. Then, I told him. "Told ya, if you believe in yourself, you can do anything. You have it in you."

He almost smiled back at me. And, suddenly it felt like a swarm of butterflies flooding me and picking me up over to the human houses where the angels would sing upon my arrival. And the humans would swat at me, but I would dodge them with my amazing tricks and I'd be the hero of my colony. I'd destroy the tree, and ban the pact. And, the soaring of flies would be real again, not just some dream.

"So, can we go?" I asked enthusiastically, just imagining the sunshine smiling back at me similar to that day so long ago.

But, there was a frown on Frons' face. "Volare, wouldn't you rather like to rest in the hospital room instead of flying what could be a treacherous trip?"

"I have never been one to relax. To me, it's always been about adventure. Why spend your life just relaxing, all bored? You should take some risks or at least have fun. Sitting in the flirmiary is no fun at all. You can't see the neighborhood or smell it."

"Smell it?" he asked.

"Yeah," I replied, "I like to smell food. You know, if I can't eat it."

Frons stared, either speechless or unsure of what to say.

"So are we going now?" I asked.

Frons gave me another frown. "Fine, but don't blame me if we end up in the belly of a bird."

All I could do was stare at him in shock. What was so traumatic in his life that he was this against flying? Is everyone in my colony like this? I have to ensure that he gains some perseverance and the inspiration to take to the skies. Maybe, I'll just make him into a bird. A tiny, black bird with green eyes and a net. Oh, how funny is that.

As I held onto Frons's back, he started to flap his wings. But, after his one second flight, he abruptly stopped. He turned to me, "Are you sure you want to do this? Imagine how your parents will react? And not to mention, we'll get in trouble with the colony. They might limit your sightings."

I sighed. "That's true, but I'd rather visit the houses and never see them again, then have to stare at them, just knowing I can't go. I have been dreaming this my whole life ever since we made that pact. I just want to taste it one more time and enjoy the smell before my parents ban me for eternity."

Frons sighed. I knew what he was thinking. It was what everyone thought. Whenever I told other flies about my dream and how I hated our pact, it was always the same expression. *That fly is crazy. Why would she want to leave when it's safe here? Doesn't she know of the invisible insecticide? Does she want to make her life shorter? Why make your life shorter? Why make your life shorter? Why make your life shorter...*

I stared at the blurry visions of the neighborhood, as something started to cloud my vision. I heard a familiar voice. A male voice. I shook my head, gaining vision as I realized Frons was calling my name. I shook my head one last time to clear the thoughts before I crawled on Frons' back and he started flapping his wings away from this cursed tree. Slowly by slowly, we escaped the shadow of the tree. I looked back one last time, that mixed feeling of right and wrong. Although I was happy, there was a bit of sadness taking up one hundredth of my heart. The tree might have been keeping me captive and chained to my colony, but it still served as a nice community.

Community, not home. The tree might have been *a* home, but it was never going to be my "home home". Like I have mentioned, we are nomads. We don't have one home. We have multiple. And this time the human's home would be my temporary residence before I would fly back into reality.

Chapter 3

I turned my head to face the large pretty neighborhood in front of me. The trees were charming shades of red, orange, and green. A slight breeze blew into our faces as we flew the opposite way it was blowing. And for the first time in a long time, I let go of the hate and sadness, allowing only the happiness to overwhelm me. In fact, I was eager. Eager to explore the human houses again. Maybe even scavenge some food from there. Finally I could!

Lots of flies in our colony whine when it's their turn to scavenge. I have always volunteered to find food, but of course, my parents don't allow me. So, I sit bored in my room, just staring out into the view of what could have been.

However, now was the time I could actually accomplish what flies agreed not to do. Now, I could actually scavenge and eat the human foods. Now, I could relive my life before. Even just for a few hours.

As we began to approach higher into the skies, I thought back to my parents and that day my father and I chased each other into the bright blue sky. Most flies are color blind, but my parents always told me I was different. I could see color because I was special and unique.

Frons, traveling slower than would have been appreciated, kept looking apprehensively towards the view of the human houses. As I sat on his thorax, I felt the tiny vibrations of his front legs. Now, I just felt remorseful. Poor Frons, dragged into this because of me. But as frightened as he might have been, he did have the ability to do what I "asked" him to do.

"Which house do you want to go to?" he asked, a tremble in his voice. "I can't hold you for too long." Now I could hear the fear in his voice. Not just for flying, but accidentally dropping me. I kept my voice soft, unenthused, but I appreciated how he cared.

"Um, let me see." I extended and focused my antennae as I smelled a luxurious scent from the farthest left of this beautiful sight. "Go more left and the house is on the farthest left side."

"Wow, you can smell that good?" Frons asked, astonished.

"I think of it as my heart guiding me rather than my good sense of smell."

Frons sighed.

"What happened?" I asked. "Why do you keep sighing?" I asked, now a little irritated.

"I just don't understand you. You have this determination and focus on this goal, but are you ever going to use your head?" He took a pause, and before I could speak, he started again. "And I'm just not like that. I'm not an extrovert, I'm not focused; I just do what my parents have told me to do. They've told me that the human houses are dangerous, so I've listened to them and forbidden myself to go. And, right now, I'm just afraid. Afraid of the insecticide, of the humans, and the predators zooming in every direction."

"I know you are Frons…" I didn't get to finish before he went on again.

"Why aren't you the same? Why do you have to be so rebellious? Why can't you just learn to go with the flow a little? Every fly enjoyed the human food, but we'd rather be safe than sorry. And, for heaven's sake, the insecticide is frickin' invisible!"

I took a deep breath before answering. I formed the words in my brain for the first time without listening to my heart. "You're right, Frons. I am rebellious. But, I have this dream. And I know you think it's ridiculous, but it's there and I'm proud of it. And every dream has obstacles. It's not a dream if there aren't any. The best thing I can do is to not let them hold me back."

Frons flew in silence.

But I continued on, slightly changing my perspective as I began to realize the complexity of it all. "And sometimes, I don't use my head. I guess, I'm just used to my life before that any change seems... unbearable. And, so I guess I've just developed a dream in my head. But that doesn't change what I want my life to be or the lengths I'm going to go to get it."

Frons didn't say anything this time either. But, I couldn't feel a tingling feeling in his legs anymore. I think he finally got my message, and I think I finally got his. Maybe it's time I start using my head. My head for the limits, but my heart for the passion.

"You're a stubborn, but daring fly," he then told me.

I smiled, but unfortunately, he didn't see it. It didn't matter.

And through the next few moments of silence where I had made peace, there was a catastrophe to ruin it all. "Frons," I said, trying to sugarcoat it.

"Yeah?" he said, his voice finally calm.

"Don't look now, but there's a duck heading toward us at 3 o'clock."

"Wait what?" he turned towards me.

I abruptly stuck my hand out, panic in me. "Duck on the right!" I shrieked.

"Duck?" he said with confusion. Suddenly, he lowered his head as if ducking.

"No! There's a duck to your right!" I yelled again, frantically pointing and tapping his back. He immediately turned his noggin only to see a duck sailing towards us. I couldn't tell if the duck saw us, but it was definitely headed towards us.

"What do I do?!" he whimpered, and all of a sudden, I became worried, too. It almost felt like my life was about to flash once again until the time where I'd actually make it to the Underworld. And, I couldn't help but contemplate how my life had all been pointless.

Wait a minute. What the heck am I saying? My life hasn't been pointless; instead, it's been wondrous and amazing and purposeful. I deserve to live and I deserve to be happy and follow my passion. So, without doubting myself any further, I took charge of the situation and helped calm a panicking fly down. Seriously, I yelled at Frons to go down. "Go down! Go down!" I shrieked.

He pulled down, but the bird came down, too, suddenly locking eyes on its lunch.

"Go faster!" I buzzed.

"If I could go faster, don't you think I would?!"

"The bird's gaining on us!"

"I told you this was dangerous. We're about to become fly stew!"

"Here, just follow my instructions," I told him. "Slow down as the bird nears us, then immediately turn down."

"I can't easily dodge a large bird!" he shrieked.

I thought about how I could calm him down. "Listen, you're a fly, so just fly. I'll guide you away from the bird, but all you need to do is keep on flying and be confident in yourself."

Frons took a breath as he calmed down. "Okay, guide the way."

"Okay, just slow down." The bird started to speed up towards us. "Now, in three seconds, immediately fly down."

"Okay," Frons replied, still terrified.

"One, two, three!" I yelled. The bird's beak just barely touched my abdomen, but all of a sudden, Frons jerked down, leaving the bird hurtling forwards.

"Woo-hoo!" I said. "Oh my *flyness*, amazing job, Frons!"

"Thanks," he said. However, just when we were about to celebrate, the bird flew down, facing us again. Frons immediately flashed forward, but it didn't make much of a difference.

"Wow, that bird never quits," I said.

"What do I do now?" he asked, starting to panic all

over again. His voice quivered and I could feel apprehension tingling in his legs.

I looked forward to see if there was any obstacle the bird couldn't cross through. As the neighborhood zoomed into view, I spotted a few shrubs that'd be perfect as a hiding place. "Okay, just speed up, and hide in that shrub right there. The bird's beak should hopefully lose us in there."

"Okay." Frons started to flap his wings harder, but he still went at the same speed. Meanwhile, the bird was gaining on us. "I told you I'm not a bird. I can't soar."

I took a deep breath. "Look, Frons, just like before, you have to believe in yourself. Just open your heart and persevere as you fly faster. If you try, we can escape this bird."

Frons closed his eyes for a while as he remained in thought. Then he took a deep breath. "Fine, I'll try." He flapped his wings harder, and began to murmur. I smiled. Finally, I had spread a little courage to someone else.

He continued to flap and flap and brought his front legs forward, pushing them back while hurtling his body forward. He added in his head movement, and after a while, it looked awkward, but all I could do was smile.

However, Frons was not smiling. Instead, he was focusing his entire mind on driving through the cool breeze swirling around us and into the small shrub's opening. He was gripping me tighter as the shrub was nearing closer. Then, he abruptly bolted, entering the bush with the leaves acting as ninjas and trying to attack us. I closed my eyes and held on to Frons as he flew all the way deep inside. I opened my eyes when he was all the way, deep into the shrub and had finally stopped and caught his breath. In fact, I could hear his deep breathing. But, I didn't lecture him any further. I simply stayed silent as the bird approached the bush, stuck its beak in, and then left, having lost its prey.

Finally, we were able to cheer upon the bird's leave. Our wings buzzed and despite our size, it felt like the whole Earth could hear our happy screams. "Oh my flyness, Frons! You seriously flew that! I knew you could do it!"

He smiled. "Yeah, I guess."

I just stared at him. I was going to talk to him further, pressuring him to fully acknowledge what he did, but instead, I remained quiet. I'll simply let him enjoy himself in his own way.

Pretty soon, Frons flapped his wings, heading out of the bush, and then turned to face the neighborhood. "Where was the house again?"

"All the way to the farthest left."

"That's going to take a while, though," Frons complained.

"It's worth it, I promise you."

Frons shook his head as he flew towards our destination. Meanwhile, I cherished the view of the neighborhood. What could have been turned into what did happen. I beamed. Finally, my wish would come true. Finally, I could do what I'd been longing to do — what I'd been imagining myself doing since that pact. Finally. Finally. Finally…

Frons shook his head as he flew towards the destination. This time, his body was stable, but loosened and although I couldn't actually see his face, I could tell that he was sailing through the wind. His wings moved him forward, but passion is actually what propelled him. As I guided him along the way, he eventually entered the backyard of the exact house I had smelled. I faced the ugly walls of the house. It was just red and gray.

We had arrived. We had arrived. We had arrived at the house. I couldn't believe it. We had seriously arrived. Is this all just a dream? Is it a joke? Is it all just my imagination playing tricks on me? Or maybe just a good dream. But, This can't be real, can it? I was once here, but then there, stuck in the horrid tree, and back here again. This can't be real.

"Well, Volare, looks like you got what you wanted," Frons replied, staring at the house with glee.

"Thanks a lot," I said, myself still staring at the boring plain bricks of the house. "I can't actually believe I'm here once again. We traveled all the way from the tree to this house."

He laughed. "Yeah, we did."

"This ride really benefited you," I remarked.

"Yeah, I guess it did." What was with all the "I guess I

did's?" He should be celebrating himself right now.

"My name will finally be in use," I said, and I let myself fall into the vague breeze as he landed on a bench.

I looked around the backyard. There was a beautiful garden there and a bunch of plants. However, as I looked closer, I noticed some of the plants had been chomped off. Flies must've scavenged for food here, I thought.

Suddenly, a zap of worry rushed through my body. I was filled with happiness and glory, but I also had a bad feeling. And I rarely did. All I could do was speculate the invisible insecticide. What if the humans had sprayed insecticide after we chomped off their leaves?

Frons turned to look at me. "What happened? I thought you were happy to come here," he asked.

I took a sigh and a deep breath. "Of course I am. I'm the happiest I could've ever been. I guess now... I'm just nervous, and to be honest, scared. I haven't done this in a while," I paused. "And, what if they have insecticide?" I swallowed my spit.

Frons didn't give the response I was looking for. "Oh, come on, you made me fly all the way here. So, you better be a big girl and face your fears."

I stared at him. What cringy advice was that?

He started laughing. "Look, you told me to avoid obstacles. So, I guess you'll just have to believe in yourself and try. You said it yourself, 'it's worth it.'" I simply nodded, and shook off any fear I had of the insecticide. Because there wouldn't be any. There can't: I came this far.

Frons grabbed a hold of me and started to flap his wings through the door that was ajar. Once we were inside, I stared down at the table. And, oh my flyness, there was a whole feast there!

Frons landed on the table and set me down. However, something happened. It was Frons. His body started to swirl around and his wings started to close. Wait, what was going on? His body was shaking. No, I've had this moment before. No, no, this can't be happening. No, there can't be insecticide. I came this far. He came this far. We're not going down. But, he fell off the table before I could do anything, and my eyes started to fog. I felt myself shaking and everything was faint. The insecticide was… taking… over. And just like that, I couldn't see anything; I was just lost in an eternal abyss. Everything was dark. I was trapped in the feeling of death.

I never should've come here. I should've forgotten about the humans and their food. I should've left this impossible passion behind. No passion is worth doing with an impossible obstacle. I could've been safe. Safe with my parents, on the leaf, near them. Who cares if they have lost their adventure? Now, I have died. Now, I am dead. Now, I will never see the light of day again.

Worst of all, I took Frons with me. I was the reason for the death of another fly because I was too impatient to wait for my own wing to heal. I had ignored my aunt's and uncle's death before, focusing only on my inability to visit the human houses versus the horror of their death. I never felt any feelings towards them but instead towards the privilege being robbed from me. But now, I felt it. And, all I could focus on was how I had killed him and killed myself.

"Uh, so are you ready?" Frons asked.

I shook my head, regaining consciousness of the world around me. I was still in the backyard. Frons looked concerned as I peered around. "Are you okay?" he asked.

"What?" I said, immediately turning to him. "I'm fine," I finally said. "I think I just was daydreaming." I scrunched my face as I shook off my jitters.

"Fly jitters?" Frons asked. "You're worried about the insecticide?"

I took a deep breath. "You know when I said you have to avoid the obstacles?"

"Yeah…?"

"But, this obstacle, it's unavoidable. It's invisible, for god's sake. So how am I supposed to know if it's there? The humans have created lots of new things over the past years."

"Oh, come on. We got this far. Well, I did. You helped me understand to believe in oneself and focus on what the heart is guiding, not the bunch of criticism the head gives. I guess you'll just have to hope for the best. Remember, it's 'worth it.' So be the adult fly you are and get over it."

I smiled in annoyance. He was using my own advice against me. And what was that about me being a big girl? Looks like he's finally gained confidence. I laughed at his response.

But, suddenly, even though I was ready to go, he wasn't. Oh, come on, not the frickin' same thing again. "Volare, I have to tell you something."

"Yeah?" I asked.

"My best friend was actually like you."

"Excuse me?" I asked. I'm sorry, what did he just say? I think I am unique and the only kind of myself.

"Well, she might've not been as dedicated as you are — you are something else — but she was very passionate about human food. And well, she died." He took a pause. "A human killed her. Not a bird, not the insecticide, but a human."

I couldn't find anything to say to him. Instead he continued on, "Guess she might've not been the good flier she thought she was. And the second the insecticide threat came out, I convinced myself to never go anywhere dangerous again. But, you changed that."

I beamed, and there was a moment of silence before I said, "I'm sorry about her." And then I got moody. "You know, I just realized how my aunt and uncle had died of insecticide. And I am suddenly wondering how I never mourned them. I mean, they died. I maybe cried for a second and then I complained about the insecticide and the tree without giving a damn that they were gone. I mean, who was I?"

"You were Volare. Don't be hard on yourself."

"No, it was like I loved human food more than my own aunt and uncle."

"You didn't love them any less. You were just distracted. It's okay, that was in the past."

I beamed at Frons. "Wow, you really know how to make me feel better."

Frons nodded. He gave a smile as he grabbed a hold of my thorax and started to flap his wings through the crack in the door. I took a deep breath. Let's do this again. The positive way. I turned my head to face the sky like I had seen humans do when in need of help. Whoever was up there, please help me through this situation.

We made it through the doorway and into the home. So far, so good. We passed farther into the home, trying to make it to where the food was kept. Slow and steady.

Frons glided into the hallways, careful not to make a buzz and alarm the humans. As we passed into another room, I smelled delicious food. Frons flew downward and into the room, landing on the table. I eagerly let go of him and approached the food, taking a small nibble. Oh, it tastes delicious! Much better than leaves! Frons joins in, too, and he couldn't help but smile at the experience he was having right now. Maybe now, he realized my true inspiration for obsessing over human foods.

The portions were huge, and I could've drowned myself

in the sauces, but I'd rather not be too smelly going back home.

Nonetheless, the great smell of the food erupted into my antennae, and my hypopharynx had a workout liquefying and swallowing everything. My wings buzzed and buzzed, but I honestly didn't care. They were flapping with joy. Even my broken wing fluttered in the cool air flowing through the house. I circled the plates, swallowed the luscious human food which I kept in my mouth for as long as I could before it was finally time to leave. We had been there long enough, and the sun was starting to set.

I motioned towards Frons, and right then and there, the humans came back. I was wondering where they were. As soon as they entered the room containing the foods, they spotted us and that was when they released the easiest weapons possible. Their hands. They started swatting at the food and where we were perched right as Frons gripped me tightly on his back and swerved around a human hand. Phew, that was very close. Another millimeter and we'd probably be squished. Dead as an insect. But, Frons had gained his confidence and the anticipation of what would happen when we arrived back at the tree only left him more worried and impatiently wanting to return. He sped through the hall as the humans soon gave up and then out the open backyard door. Then, he sailed into the air, through the breeze, through the smiling sunset in the distance, and off across the field to the tree so far ahead.

As he flew, I quickly buzzed, "Thank you so much,

Frons."

"Oh, it was no problem."

"What? Of course it was. Do you remember that bird?"

Frons laughed. "Yeah, maybe it was a problem, but it had a good solution and result. It helped the both of us."

Yeah, it did, I told myself. It helped me too. That part I can completely agree on.

Chapter 4

As soon as we came speeding through my room's hole, my parents were waiting there. I avoided staring at them as Frons landed and set me down. He then smiled at me, and levitated away.

"Where were you?!" my mother shrieked as soon as Frons had left.

I honestly was not sure how to word this. "I went traveling."

"Traveling?! Your wing is broken!" she stared at my wing, making sure there was still a rip. And, there was. A small rip in my right wing.

"Another fly held me while we flew," I told her, clearing up the confusion.

She was horrified and speechless.

"That fly who left?" my father asked, being protective. "Is he in this colony?"

"Yeah, he is."

"Where did you guys go?" my mother asked. "Wait, never mind, you obviously went to a human house, didn't you, Volare?" she said.

I took a while before responding. "Yes, I did." My mother was just about to pounce on me, before I spoke again. "But there wasn't any insecticide. And the humans didn't come until after we left."

"Yeah, well, duh, there wasn't any insecticide because you came back safely, but the whole human house is dangerous. You think it's safe because of this experience, but it won't be the next time," my mother replied.

I didn't know what else to say. "Mom, it's fine. We came back safe. It was all good. And guess what? Frons and I outran a bird."

"A bird was chasing you?!" my mother shrieked again.

"Who's Frons?" my father asked.

"He's the other fly that traveled with me."

"And, you seriously outran a bird?" he asked me.

I nodded. I saw something change on my father's face. Suddenly, his eyes reflected upon my great feat, and for just a moment, it seemed like he was reliving the moment. I don't know if his eyes turned blue, or maybe it was just the sun through the window, but I was hoping that maybe he would change his mind about the pact. It was a huge hope from just a second long gaze, but I really hoped.

"We got to soar," I added, smiling. Maybe the word "soar" would change things.

And, I was right. Something did change. My father smiled. "Volare got to soar," he said. Then, he turned to my mother. "You know, we've lost our sense of adventure. Volare's right. She has been right for a long time. We're flies. So, we have to fly."

My mother almost scoffed. "Yeah, we do fly. We scavenge for food and we fly around this tree, which keeps us safe."

My dad just stared at her, but she didn't say anything furthermore. After a few seconds, she said, "Look, the thought of flying and soaring — she pointed at me — might seem compelling and you know, fun, but it definitely isn't safe."

"Mom," I started, but she continued to speak.

"No, it isn't. We have no reason to make our short lives shorter. Insecticide, predators, the humans, nature in general. And having multiple homes is downright ridiculous and tiresome."

All my dad and I could do was simply stare at her. She stared at us with a fierce look. Even when I was a young fly, my mom had always been a stubborn and opinionated fly. But, this time was different. This time, I had my father on my side, and I had the feat of avoiding the insecticide and flying across the whole neighborhood. All of it worked. The reflection in his eyes and the pleading look on my face eventually wore her out. She took a deep breath, and finally gave up. "Yeah, I know. We have lost our adventure." She looked at me and then my father. "Those times were incredible and fun, and they may have been risky, but what's the point of life if you don't take risks." She looked at me, nudging me. "We have short lives, so we should enjoy them."

My father gave a smile and embraced her. I tried, but due to my broken wing, my body just ached.

Then, my mother turned to me. "So, about that fly."

"Oh, mom," I said, laughing.

Epilogue

My wings healed in a couple of weeks. They were the longest weeks of my life, but I got through it. There was plenty more to do. Frons told his parents about the flight, and although horrified at first, they eventually understood. Our families met, and we worked to remove this pact once and for all. I like to say I was the ambassador; after all, this whole thing started with me. We spent a while convincing all the flies in our colony to drop the pact. This was not easy at all.

They complained and whined and were even worse than my parents before. Of course, since they were the majority, our pact didn't drop so easily. Arguments were held every day. The flies protested that the neighborhood wasn't safe, the insecticide wasn't safe, and therefore leaving the tree for fun should be the furthest thing from anyone's mind. I helped with this argument; Frons did, too. He and I explained how listening to one's heart trumps their head. We explained how to gain confidence in ourselves and follow the passions that make us flies. I shared the longing I had felt during those days stuck in a prison. "My heart beat towards the neighborhood, my antennae extended forward to smell the luscious foods, and all I knew was that I had to escape this prison to try those human foods once again. To sail across the skies as the sun sets. The tree might protect us, but in the same way, it's condemning us. We're stuck here. We're flies, but we're not flying. We have short lives, and risks will make it shorter, but enjoyment will allow us to get through it," I told them. And after weeks and weeks of arguments and agreements, the pact was finally withdrawn.

I could simply scream all my happiness out. I was thrilled; convincing my parents to see the light of the day was a lot different than influencing change in all of these flies.

The next few days, the flies of the colony separated into their families and took off through the large hole in the tree. Most of them looked back at the stationary home they were leaving, but others sailed off, through the fields and through the skies, representing the microscopic species of the neighborhood.

I soared up above anyone else with Frons' family and mine. The sun was there, right above me, and the clouds pushed me forward. And I smiled. I smiled. And smiled. We zoomed in and out of human houses, stealing quick tastes of the human food before the humans chased us out of their homes. And, unfortunately, we lost a few flies. We weren't sure if it was insecticide or a bird, but it's okay. That's selfish to say, but it really is okay. It was just their time to leave. They had all their fun.

Finally, for the first time in a long time, I got to soar. I got to be Volare. I got to tease the humans. I got to outrun the predators, who gave up after a few seconds. I got to fly. Just fly with my parents through the bright skies, the sun dawning on us and the wind sailing past our wings. Just fly. Just fly. Just fly…

Like Gold

Afternoon had finally approached in the huge, white playroom. The little humans inched towards their parents. I watched from my uncomfortable position on the floor as the parents took the little, crying creatures away to give their yawning faces a rest. Adrenaline overwhelmed me with each step the parents took away from me. Until, at last, there was a good distance between us.

Now, I can be free. Now, I can be what I am meant to be.

A shiny, dancing monkey.

I stretched my feet in front of me. My body wiggled and I shook out my hands. My eyes targeted the pole next to me, and pretty soon, I found myself leaping from it onto the beanbag in the middle of the playroom. It was a dangerous flight, but monkeys make it happen.

"Come on, everybody! Let's wiggle around as the humans have left and we are safe and sound!" I babbled with my annoying monkey tune that I did every day.

I performed a back flip on the beanbag that I was on, and pretty soon, my hips started moving. I started busting out moves. All the furry, little animals separated and thrown under blocks and on top of tables approached me, probably thrilled to see my sick dance moves.

"Look, the golden monkey thinks his dancing is gold," an animal joked. Everyone laughed in response as parrots mimicked and toucans guffawed. I rolled my eyes in a sarcastic way, but tried my best not to grimace for real.

Gold, such a shiny, such a beautiful object, was sadly my color. Of course, it was beautiful on me, and I wasn't against looking good, but being gold brought along other... expectations.

To state the obvious, I am a golden stuffed monkey that the babies play with. I am always left pondering about why I was created with golden material, but all of the other animals had felt the need to joke about it. Suddenly, the greatness of gold stitched into me and I was expected to become good and talented at everything. I always smiled and laughed along with them whenever they compared my skills to my looks, but it never seemed amusing to me. But, to be fair, my dance moves are incredible; my leadership skills are a league of their own.

While my hip continued moving and my arms started swaying, the other animals joined in. They loosened their bodies after the hours of lying frozen in the same position in some corner. A bear busted out the Orange Justice, and a parrot started shouting out lyrics to a random song. A turtle put on some headphones and pretty soon became our DJ as he played explosive music on his tiny speakers. Despite the loud music and our yelling, I wasn't worried for a second. Humans weren't able to hear our voices since our mouths were made of cotton and other fabrics. Yes, they probably could've seen us dancing with our little arms and legs, but why would they check the playroom out of the blue?

The party had just started, but the bad news just needed to seep in. I was used to this by now, but I was really hoping it wouldn't be true this time.

"Austie is missing!" a macaw hollered.

The music quit with a sudden fade, the turtle's headphones fell off to the side, and everyone's eyes turned to the macaw who had ended their awesome party. The macaw started to go pink in his yellow feathers before nodding his head to confirm his statement.

The next thing I heard was a groan from each animal before I turned to face my sister. She shrugged her shoulders apologetically and gave me the innocent look she tried every day. Again, my baby brother Austie had snuck away from her sight; because of his frequent actions, I no longer had felt the need to be angry.

Upon hearing that your own baby brother is missing, anxiety would consume you, but there was one fact: he wasn't missing. He was simply dragged by the horrible nature of mischief. Austie, despite his shimmery self, loved shiny and unique objects like jewelry and antiques. Fortunately for him, this house is filled with it. Right now, the chances of him stuck in one of the jewelry closets, tossing around necklaces and rings to his liking are high.

So, after the news stumbled upon my ears and sunk in, I simply took a deep breath like I always did and replied to the whole community in front of me, "Well, we all know where

Austie is, so we should probably get him before he is discovered by the parents."

My community wasn't happy. They started shouting out complaints. I tried to calm them with my arm motions, but after failed attempts, I just spoke, "Yeah, yeah. We are all tired of having to maintain Austie, but guess what? He is little. He is learning, and he needs guidance. And we definitely need to get him so the parents don't discover him and call stuffed animal control or whatever about a stealing monkey." I could tell my audience wasn't relieved, so I gave them the confirmation they needed, calming their selfish personalities. "I understand how you all might not want to look for him, and that's fine. *I* am his older brother, and it's *my* responsibility to look after him. I will go retrieve him before he causes any more damage. After all, he's just in a jewelry closet. There's one right there."

I didn't hear any more complaints from the animals after my speech. Instead, I focused on the jewelry closet outside the playroom, no worry filling me up because I had nothing to worry about.

I jumped off of my beanbag, over a couple of blocks, and swung from some more poles meant for the babies. In a few seconds, I landed onto the handle of the jewelry closet door, just as my tiny fingers tried to open it.

My body hung from the door handle as everyone watched. I was used to this, having to do it almost everyday, so within another few seconds, I had opened the door. The blackness of the closet's wall and the shininess of the jewelry revealed just what I needed.

***

Yup, emptiness was what I just needed. Absolutely not.

As I stared at the dozens of jewelry but zero tiny monkeys, my heart started to beat fast even though the only heart I had was probably just a ball of cotton My sister spoke from below, "Brother? What is it?"

"He — he isn't here."

"Austie?" my sister asked. "Then, where is he?"

"I — I don't know, Audrey." My voice trembled and my eyes didn't leave the sight I was witnessing. Pretty soon, my sister swung up onto the door handle and shock overwhelmed her, too. "Oh my god, Austie isn't here."

The other animals gasped in the background and began to murmur between themselves. "But, where would he be then?" a dog asked.

"Not here, apparently," a cat purred.

More of the animals started to talk, but I couldn't muster a sound. It was almost like my mouth was frozen, frozen like I was in the Arctic instead of this warm house on a sunny day.

"So, what do we do?" an animal asked. "Should we go look for him?" Although I wasn't facing the animal who asked that, I was one hundred percent sure that the other animals in the playroom would probably be trying to cover the animal's mouth who said that. But I simply made it easier for them.

"No, it's okay. Audrey and I will go find him. There are more closets to search, so it may take time, and I don't want anyone wasting their own." The animals were appeased.

Just as I gazed at Audrey and she nodded her head, a salamander shouted, "Wait a minute!" All the animals turned to the salamander who shouted that, probably furious as we faced the tiny thing. "Give the monkey a break! He helps us all the time, leading us and maintaining our parties and we're not giving anything back! Even if he isn't asking for our help, we should still provide it."

All I could do was beam at his words as the faces on each of the animals' slowly changed. It was from anger to consideration. The salamander came closer to me. "We will help you two find Austie. After all, he is part of us."

After a few seconds, the other animals stared at my desperate face. They stared at my worried and begging eyes. And since they were pretty fickle and easy to convince, they joined in. A toucan shouted, "Go golden monkey!" The cats purred, the dogs barked, and the parrots mimicked what the salamander had said while the macaw started shouting Austie's name.

Through it all, Audrey looked at me with love in her eyes and I shouted out encouraging words to my faithful community right before we started our search for Austie.

We had one goal: find Austie. However, searches don't

always go as planned, and this one definitely didn't. From a hearty search came a huge truth about me and my siblings. While we were all simple, golden stuffed monkeys at first, we became something much more.

***

All the lazy animals checked under blocks and several of the baby mats, but there wasn't any little golden monkey hidden anywhere. After waiting and more waiting, I finally convinced the animals to move on from the playroom and search elsewhere. I was hundred percent sure that he wouldn't have been hiding there and avoiding our party in the process.

With my sister and I leading the way, we took a bear to act as a good base and a salamander to stand on top of my sister, me, and the bear to check a closet. Only, there was no little monkey there either.

We tiptoed into another room, keeping eyes on the balcony railing as the humans were out of our sight. Phew. We checked another closet with same formation from before; our eyes searched under other objects in the room. But, there was no stuffed monkey there either.

***

I don't know if an hour or more was spent finding Austie with no avail, but guilt crept into my body. The optimism and certainty from before no longer sprouted inside of me. I felt horrible. I could breathe, but at the same time, it was like I couldn't.

My own baby brother was missing, and it was entirely my fault. I should've taken the responsibility to watch him, not my sister. She could've led the party and I could've done what my job was: be a devoted, elder brother.

"Could he be downstairs?" the salamander asked. "Downstairs?" I repeated. My heart skipped a beat. Downstairs? Austie downstairs? He's never gone there before. We've never gone there before. No, he can't. He can't be downstairs. But, then again, he was a mischievous and fast-learning little monkey. Anything could go with him.

Just as I was thinking about this new idea, my sister approached me, "August?" I turned to her. "I'm so sorry. I'm really sorry this time." Looking at her, I think there were tears in her eyes.

"No, no —" I started.

She cut me off and resumed talking, "No, I am sorry. I shouldn't have just let him go off again. Honestly, I wasn't that worried this time when I was watching him because I thought it would be the same as always, but I was wrong. And, now, who knows where he is? I am so deeply sorry." She took a pause; there was a tremble in her voice.

But, she continued on. "However, I believe we'll find him. Remember what mother said. We're gold on the outside because we're gold on the inside. Gold is pure, beautiful just like our sibling hood is."

I started to speak, but she cut me off again. "I know you

don't believe in the whole talk of being gold but I believe there was a reason why we were made this way. It's like a symbol of strength and purity even though ironically gold isn't the strongest thing on Earth. But I feel like it has provided us a purpose and has connected the three of us."

I guess today was national speech day. It seemed like everyone was on a roll with their words. I desperately wanted to tell my sister how wrong she was, but I didn't have the heart to do so. After all, at least one of us should keep faith since faith is apparently beside me. So, I just smiled. I gave her a pat on the back, and I moved on from the talk of gold. "So, sis, do you think Austie is downstairs?"

She gave it a thought. "Honestly, monkeys learn fast, especially Austie. He probably could've managed."

That was not the answer I was hoping for. I almost grunted or made a sound of exasperation until a cat came up to me and asked, "How was the search?"

I tried not to roll my eyes and simply responded, "Well, we haven't found Austie and we think he is downstairs."

"Downstairs?! Good grief, I am not going there!" As soon as the cat yelled that, the other animals in the back all shouted "Downstairs?!" in agony.

I took a deep breath and responded, "Yes, downstairs. And, it's okay. Audrey and I will go, so none of you have to worry."

I heard a *phew* from many of the animals right before

the salamander dared to open his mouth again. "Now, wait just a minute!"

This time I was facing the brave little thing, and I saw the animals' subtle glares as the salamander started to speak. "What are we if we don't help them?"

The cat seemed to find some absurdity about this and spoke, "What do you mean? We already helped them."

The salamander snorted. "You? You did nothing. And neither did anyone else. Only the four of us actually checked places." He pointed to me, my sister, the bear, and himself. "Even if you did, why can't you help him more? We don't always have to need something; we can simply be selfless. And, anyways, August takes risks for us at parties, so we can put our fears aside and help him. It's not like going downstairs is dangerous. It's just something new for us."

A pause. Hesitation. A glare. More hesitation. Contemplation.

These were the steps the animals took before trotting down by my side to where the staircase was. The cats, their lazy selves, stayed back. A few came, but a few stayed. And, I honestly didn't care. I had the majority with me; that was all I needed.

As soon as we approached the staircase, my first look was down. The animals stared down. And, they stared at the huge size of each of the steps, and the millions of steps to go. "May be this was a bad idea," the salamander whispered to himself.

It was scary indeed. But, I imagined it different. I imagined it like a tree in the jungle. Daunting, dangerous, but inviting. Yes, it was inviting me to take a charge and swing from one of the vines to the bottom. Where Austie was.

I could feel the jungle wind, the voices of squeaks, footsteps, and so many animals in the background, with the green of the leaves, of the grass, and the dark gold of the sand in some places. *Gold.* Suddenly, I remembered Audrey's so-called speech. Although I wanted to argue, I took a breath and decided to pay some importance to her words.

"Okay, ready guys?" I turned to each of the animals as we tiny things formed a huge clump.

The animals all shook their heads. The salamander whispered no. The cats stayed back, probably regretting their decision to follow me.

I took another deep breath and turned to them. "Guys, this is scary. I know. But think of it differently. Think of it as an adventure in a jungle or a savanna or the Arctic, wherever you're from. Think of it like a quest. Think of it as a way of unlocking your true selves since of course our stuffed animal selves will never explore the outside world." They were still all very frightened. I continued, "I think of it as a jungle where monkeys are. To me, it's a huge tree, and on the bottom lies the thing to my happiness: my brother Austie. Just imagine something important to you and you will find the courage to go forward."

There was still hesitation, and underneath it, fear. Strong fear. I couldn't blame them. After all, I had more motivation than any of them. They were doing this for me, their leader, but I was doing this for my brother. I think family trumps friends. So, I just emphasized my last sentence. "Guys, just imagine some family member or someone you love is trapped downstairs and they need you to help them escape."

"It doesn't work that way, though," a leopard said. I stared at him, almost asking the question *why?* He continued on, "We were all ripped away from our family members when we were bought, and our brains know that there is no one we love downstairs so imagining it is difficult. For you, that's different. You have Austie, so excuse us for being less motivated than you."

I took a deep breath. "Yeah, I know. I'm sorry. It's fine, I'll just go." I stared at the sight, and took a step forward, starting to lift my leg up from the ground and jump onto the next huge step. Only, the animal next to me stopped me. She stared down and came right next to me. I, shocked at what she did, watched as everyone soon followed. And, then, the only thing was left was the horrific journey down the huge staircase.

Jump, crawl, jump, I went. I held on to the railings a few times and tried to swing from them. The other animals did what they pleased, but probably a million hours later, we finally arrived at the bottom. The animals were shaken by the feat they had just accomplished, but I kept my focus on finding Austie.

I couldn't risk getting side-tracked.

I thoughtlessly took a random left and came to the entryway of the parents' bedroom. I figured there must be some unique objects in here. We kept the salamander on guard, and the rest of us hurried inside. There was no monkey swinging off of poles upon our entrance, but our search didn't end well, either. Austie wasn't there.

All I wanted to do was cry. I think a tear even fell down my furry cheek, but I really just wanted to lock the door and bawl my eyes out. But, I couldn't. I had to find him, and I still had the whole house left to check.

I led the group of animals out the door where the salamander waited. "August?" he said.

"What happened?" I asked.

"Look," he held something in his hand. Something of a shimmery yellowish-brown color that was small and soft.

Stuffed animal fur. Yellow-brown stuffed animal fur.

No, wait, not brown.

It was...

"Golden fur," my sister replied,

"Could it be Austie's?" the salamander asked.

"No, it could also be ours'," my sister replied.

"No, we are made so that we don't shed any fur," I replied. "Only someone who is being played with recklessly will shed fur like that. And the only other person with golden fur is Austie." I suddenly realized exactly what I had said. I stared right at my sister as concern filled her eyes.

"Could Austie be in trouble?" she asked.

I quickly looked to the salamander. "Was there any more fur?"

"Um, I don't know. Let me check." He crawled over the floor and suddenly stopped. "Oh, yes, there's more. There's a few more specks of fur leading that way," he pointed to the hallway beyond the staircase.

"That must be where Austie is then," I said. I faced the salamander and told him, "My sister and I will go find him. I want you to fill in all the other animals. Tell some to hide here and some to go back up so that if the humans do go to the playroom, they don't become suspicious. But, I might need some backup so keep some down. Got it?" The salamander nodded his head, and I replied with a thank you.

Then I turned to my sister and the two of us followed the subtle trail of the golden fur to where I was hoping Austie lay, still unharmed and his energetic self. In the background, I heard the salamander's voice.

***

I found Austie. On a table. A high table.

He just lay there, frozen and lifeless like we all did when there were humans around us. I saw something white on his body and I realized that it was cotton sticking out. "Is that a cut?" I asked my sister. She responded with a dire yes. "We've got to get him. Are there any humans around?" My sister shook her head.

I jumped onto the fireplace as I found a lamp to swing off of. Pretty soon, I had landed on the table that held Austie. His eyes didn't move, and suddenly I had a worrying thought in my brain: *what if he isn't alive?*

While I was desperately hoping this was not the case, I whispered the loudest I could, "Austie?"

He budged. I thanked the Monkey Gods. "August?" He looked up at me. He suddenly got up and gave me a hug. "Brother August!"

Only, he soon grabbed his leg in pain. I stared at him. "Did the humans cut you?" He nodded. "Why?" I asked.

"Because, because I'm gold," he said.

I flinched at his answer. "Wait, what? What do you mean?"

"Well..." Then he started his story. He told me how he was simply lying on one of the mini-cars that the babies play with when the humans took the car and the babies away with him. "I overheard them talking to someone on the phone about us. You, me, and Audrey. We had some gold in us or something," Austie told me.

"What do you mean, we have gold?" I asked.

"Our creators put some gold in us that is worth a lot."

"In stuffed animals?"

"I guess so."

Gold? Gold in us? Is that why I've always felt the

weight of gold? Because it was in me? I thought.

"So, the humans took me and are trying to cut me up to find it. Before they take the rest of us to sell," he finished.

Suddenly, the overwhelming feeling of guilt consumed me. I was secretly agitated and disappointed when I found out Austie had snuck off again, but he hadn't. And all of us just believed he had. I also believed he had. When, in fact, he was not a slave to mischief this time but the cruelty of the humans.

"We've got to stop them," I told him. I looked down and Audrey was waiting there.

"But how?" Austie asked. "If I move from here, the humans will get suspicious, and if I don't, they will cut me and rip me apart."

"We'll come up with a plan. After all, we are like gold. I mean, we are technically gold. Gold is shiny, powerful, and beautiful just like our sibling hood is. And, we will save each other." He beamed at me as I remembered something similar that Audrey had said.

"Let's talk to the other animals," I then said. He seemed confused, so I filled him in on everything.

He was shocked at how the other animals had agreed to come down just for him. I simply smiled at him before Audrey and I followed the specks of fur back to the parents' bedroom. The salamander was waiting at the front. Upon seeing me and Audrey, he grew worried. "Did you not find Austie?"

"No, we found him, but we need everyone's help." I

called all the animals that were hidden downstairs and told them Austie's story.

"Gold. You?" an animal said with a hint of jealousy. "Like actual gold?"

"Apparently. They were trying to cut Austie to find it. I'm guessing they aren't finished since he only had one cut."

"So you want us to rescue him?" a cat purred. She was feeling envious as well.

"Yes, of course," I said, expressing the obviousness of it.

"How?" the salamander asked.

"Well, we'll figure out. We're the golden monkeys, and all of us are a wonderful community. We'll stick together and form a plan."

And we did that. We made a plan, we executed it, and we saved Austie in the end. But, it took a while. And, it was a bit crazy.

***

We had first decided to call the parents and explain to them that there wasn't actually gold in their stuffed animals, and whoever had told them before was simply joking. That way, they'd forget about Austie and put him back in the playroom. However, we soon realized that the humans couldn't hear us.

We then considered writing a note and leaving it for them, but none of us knew how to write. We could speak

English, but that's as far as we could go. And, besides, why would they listen to a random note?

So, after several blank minds and countless bad plans, some animal who I really hadn't paid attention to — a spider — opened his mouth with his beady eyes staring at me and pitched something. It might have sounded ridiculous at first, but I realized there was a possibility that it could work.

The spider said, "What if we made the humans forget about the gold?"

"What do you mean?" I asked.

"Well, I don't know, um, if we started dancing in front of them and banging drums or something, they would think they're going crazy right? Because stuffed animals are not supposed to move on their own. And then they may not come to their senses and they could faint or something. So, we will be able to take Austie away. When they wake up and they don't see Austie, they may just think they were dreaming."

I didn't answer right away. My mind was processing what the spider just said. Honestly, it didn't seem that bad compared to what we had before.

A cat said, "Haha right! Like they'd faint. That's so dumb."

"No, it's not," I said. "It could actually work. Good job."

He beamed and blended back in with the other animals.

"Let's try this, guys. What's the harm? It's not like

they're going to call the police on dancing stuffed animals."

"But how are we going to do this?" the cat asked. Then she started to sound lazy and said, "Do we have to do this?"

"No, not everyone. Some people can go back up and join the others. We only need a couple."

"Okay, fine with me." The cat turned away and started for the stairs as the other cats followed.

"Okay, well, then, Audrey, salamander, bear, spider, macaw, and the dog come with me. Everyone else you are free to go. Thanks for sticking with us."

***

Now, we marched forward. And there the humans were, their huge, superior selves. We started running across the floor just as they turned towards us.

"Are those the stuffed animals?" the man said.

"Yeah, I think so," the woman said.

"Are they moving on their own?" the man said.

"I have no idea."

Yup, we were moving on our own. And pretty soon, with fingers crossed, the humans wouldn't be moving.

I started us off. I started moving my hip and moving my fingers. The humans stared at us with scrunched eyebrows. And then, Audrey started dancing. She slid on the wooden floor with her knees just like a mop, only more graceful. The bear did the Moon Walk and the salamander did the Worm. The Macaw clapped his hands and shouted out random words even though the humans probably couldn't hear what he was saying. Lastly, the spider jumped onto the dog's back and they jumped onto a platform and then over the humans heads as the dog's paw hit the play button on the music generator the humans use.

It was a wild, chaotic cacophony as the humans were probably thinking. "Are you seeing this?" the man asked.

"Yeah, I am."

"Are we going crazy?" he asked.

"No, we can't be. Not *both* of us."

"But — but how are they doing that?"

We started to go even more crazy. Jumping onto tables and dancing as much as we could.

Pretty soon, the humans couldn't take it anymore. At least one couldn't. The man fainted and the woman knelt down to check on him. Meanwhile, the dog jumped onto the table as Austie hopped onto his back. Then the dog jumped off and galloped towards us as we all marched off back to the stairs and hurried up as fast as we could. All the woman could do was stare at us crazily and look to where her husband lay on the floor.

And, that's it. We had saved Austie. We were the golden monkeys again, part of the awesome community that were unfortunately still slaves to the babies, but we would escape one day. Sometime in the future.

We stitched Austie's cut as best as we could so it would look as if he never was cut in the first place. Luckily, the humans never came back to take him. So, we all cheered and continued with our afternoon parties. Austie stopped running away (at least for a little while) and I could finally relax.

The parties continued. They were amazing. It seemed for the first time ever, I wasn't judged for my looks. But, the animals still turned to me for everything, probably for once again, my incredible leadership skills.

Side by side, I spent as much time with my siblings as possible, finally feeling the connection that Audrey had described. But, I also felt a sense of superiority. It was just a natural sense, something that occurred for a while. I guess it came from being worth more than what I assumed I was. But, I managed to get rid of because although I wasn't the same monkey as before, I was worth the same. That's all that mattered despite the fact that I was exactly like gold.

Another Lovely

Home

Our car circled the corner and after the calm, rhythmic motion, it suddenly stopped — right in front of a large house. I hopped out of the car, tied to a leash. Against my will, my teeny legs galloped across the sidewalk until I got a whiff of an unfamiliar scent. I sniffed at it, again and again, but the smell was one that I had never experienced before. My mom held a bag in her hand as she made her way to the front door of the house, pulling me along. And all I could feel was curiosity for this unfamiliar place. What were we doing here? Should I be worried?

There was a doorbell sound that I could make out, and a few seconds later, the front door of the house opened. A woman was standing there. Involuntarily, I approached her and sniffed her foot. Her scent matched the one before, but it was still alien to me.

Then, I heard a bunch of chatter between my mom and the other woman. "I've got Cody's – that was my name –food in here, his treats, his water, food bowl, and his toys." As I looked up towards the woman, she had a bag in her hand. And it was mine. It had the smell of my toys in it and my wonderful treats. How dare this woman take what was mine. I almost shook my head. What is going on?

I struggled to take my bag from her as she spoke again. The weird sounds exiting her mouth ringed in my ears. My nose went crazy sniffing her legs and feet, but I had to. I had been brought to an unfamiliar place. And, this bag-stealer could be dangerous.

I lifted my forearms to her knees as she almost avoided coddling me unlike how most people did. And soon, I let go and hit the surface of the wooden floor just as the chatter ended. At this point, I had reached a state of complete and utter confusion, but it wasn't the same as the next moment.

The woman shortly took off my leash, escorted me inside, and waved goodbye to my mother. As she closed the door, I immediately pounced at it, sniffing at my mother's faded scent and failing to grab her departing body.

I whimpered. Had she actually left me? Was she gone?

As I turned my head to face the woman who had pulled me inside, she set down my leash and my bag on the side. Without focusing on anything else, I hurried for the bag, and stuck my face in. I desperately needed a treat right now. An amazing delicacy that could wake me up from whatever bad dream I was having.

My mouth attempted to grab the box that contained the treats, but the box's lid refused to open as I slid my nose under it. Aw, come on! All I wanted was one treat. The smells of the treats were taunting me as they sat in the box, just waiting to be eaten.

But, I soon gave up. The box was a stubborn one. I backed away from it and towards the door. All I felt myself doing was to smell from the crack so luckily there. Smell the outside world and hopefully my mom still waiting there. My nose sniffed at it, and this time I smelled absolutely nothing. I had been abandoned, probably for the millionth time in my entire life. I felt completely alone and helpless. Without my mom in reach.

I barked until I couldn't anymore. My own mother, my safe place, had actually left me. All that remained through the crack was the bland smell of the brick doorway outside the door, the light breeze of air, and maybe a wasp's nest. Yeah, I should probably stay away. Wasps do not suit dogs like me.

With nothing else to do besides deal with the solitude, I turned my attention to the woman and galloped to where she was sitting. It was a raised platform, taller than my height and positioned on weird looking legs. The best thing for me was that the woman sat there, who I was hoping could offer consolation. So, I lowered my stance and as a millisecond went by, I used the momentum of my legs to lift off from the ground. As I hit the surface of the platform, I felt the in-between feeling of comfy and rough.

The woman wasn't paying attention as I pounced up on the platform which, now that I think about, kind of reminds me of our "sofa" back home. Only that sofa was lower, perfect for my height, and felt different. Either way, a small rectangle object occupied the woman's hands and her attention. Her finger swiped on it, and her eyes didn't seem to be leaving it. But, it was fine. I could keep myself company.

I sat on the cushion there. It felt nice for my butt. And

then, she turned to me. She immediately got up, losing focus from her rectangle thing, and stared at me. Her mouth seemed to be moving, but all I could hear was jibber jabber. "Cody, please come down! Down! Don't sit on the sofa," she seemed to be saying. What did that mean? I heard my name, but nothing else.

Then, she started pointing at the ground with her finger. I stared at the carpet and then back to her. Does she want me to jump off? If I could scratch my head with my paw, I would.

But, as luck would have it, I understood what the woman was pointing to. And, all I could do was beam. Within a second I jumped off to where she was pointing to. Onto the ground and towards the treat box. I stared up at the woman with bright eyes, waiting for her to give me a treat, but instead, she sat back down. Her focus again turned to the rectangular object, and she began swiping on it with her finger.

However, I was optimistic, and I decided to guide the woman to my salvation. As I repeated my steps over to the treat box, she turned her attention to me and sauntered over. Yes! Yes! She understands I want a treat. But, she simply placed hands on my fur. She rocked her hands back and forth on my tight curls and said, "Hi, Cody. You're such a cutie," and then pet the hair on my head. No! No! I gave an annoyed grunt inside my head as my brain was starting to shut down. I didn't know what else to do at that moment.

I dug back into the treat box, and then she turned to it.

And, suddenly, my body started to become tingly and my tail shook as I saw her put one hand into the treat box. She lifted out a treat, hurrying over to the tiled floor and set it down.

That's when I gobbled it up completely. Finally! A nice, delicious beef jerky for my tummy. The taste of the treat made my stomach dance and I looked up at her to see if she would give me any more. However, she closed the treat box and set it where it was out of my reach.

Disappointed, I galloped over to where she sat, laying down on all four legs right next to her feet.

As each ticking second went by, I followed the woman all around her house: through the kitchen, into a comfy carpeted room with a huge bed, outside the bath room in which I wasn't allowed, through multiple different rooms, and back to the soft carpet near the sofa. She pet me a few times, but mostly I just followed her around through the alien hallways of her planet.

I couldn't help but notice the wide space in her house. The walls were high and filled with more rectangles and squares that had tiny humans in them. In the wide center, there was a huge screen, and suddenly I recalled this from my house. Max, Sarah, and my parents would crowd around it, and those would be the worst times for me. They would ignore me and instead watch the explosions of different shapes on the large screen.

Only, now, I can say that this is the worst time for me. They're not here: my amazing owners. To make it all worse,

I'm constantly thinking about them. And it's not happily. I imagine their faces, their hands, their food. I imagine them taking care of me, playing with me, and feeding me. Well, now it's more of me alone, standing by my food bowl, gobbling food, although they still give me those sweet, occasional pats.

Minus their forced running games, I love them. It's my duty to protect them, but how can I if they're being unfaithful to me? I've ignored their neglects, but I can't ignore this one. They left me; my mother specifically waved goodbye to me before leaving. And, I couldn't help but think now: what did all of this mean?

Was this going to be permanent? Was I supposed to stay here? Were they forever abandoning me? Were they responsible for this constant heartache and the bucket of tears exploding out of my eyes? Even if the tears weren't there, they should've been and they will be.

As I pictured the moments with my family on the large screen in front of me, I recalled what took place a few weeks ago. They had said my name "Cody" and the word "stay." To be exact, "Cody will be staying with the Johnsons," was their complete phrase although everything else was far above my comprehension. I had stayed there that day on the living room floor as they had had a discussion. I didn't understand any of it all, but I certainly don't understand my instructions now. Why were they telling me not to stay there — with them — and stay here instead?

***

I guess I never figured that the woman wouldn't be alone. Despite that weird man stuck in the room near the door behind a gray apple with a rectangle border, there were others. Children. Two of them to be exact.

I was first introduced to one of them when when I heard movement through the door near the comfy carpet — my resting point. It was a thud with a loud footstep, and as my curiosity traveled to the threshold of the door, a boy walked in the house. Before doing anything else, he came up to me and simply lowered his gaze, roughly petting me. His arms were stiff. I flinched before sniffing his moving hand and his smelly, shoe less feet as he kept his hands behind his back. His scent was almost the same as the woman's, but much more smellier. There was the strong odor coming straight from his legs.

He gave a smile, or so I thought, with a tense hand on my body. Then, he threw his bag to the side, and with his smelly feet, hurried to the sofa, stealing the woman's spot. I scurried over, staring from the worst worm's-eye view ever at him. They had indeed started to target the huge screen in front of him.

Eh, who cares? I turned to face the spot on the sofa that was free. With one push, I got on top of the sofa. Luckily, there were no complaints. At least none till later. I rested my body on top of my four legs, sowing comfort. Well, until the next child would come. The worst one.

***

Annoying sounds erupted from the large screen in front of the boy as I simply laid in the same position. The boy twiddled his thumbs on some irregular device in his hand and his hair stuck up from behind. But, everything was peaceful. I had seen most of the alien house, but this spot was one of the best. The whole aura of the room seemed to suit me. And, with this amazing comfort I was feeling, I really thought I could forget the whole abandonment thing. But, it turns out even the worst things so deeply attempted to ignore comes back to haunt you. And no matter how hard you try to forget some things, you can't. The brain just keeps throwing the moments back at you like darts on a dartboard.

A loud footstep disturbed my restful ears. Boom! Boom! Well, in truth, they only disrupted my serenity and seemed loud.   I lifted my noggin and immediately pounced off the couch. I darted towards the location of the sound. The door. The door near my favorite spot.

And the person who would come through would surely remind me of heartbreak.

A girl opened the door. From her dark brown hair, average height, and existence, Sarah came to my mind. Sarah. The daughter of my owners. I couldn't describe her as anything else but the best. The most sympathetic. The second person to go to if I couldn't curl up in my mother's lap, or happily and peacefully lay on the rug. And here, a doppelganger of her stood right in front of me, her big brown eyes staring sweetly into mine, and her hands reaching to pet my tight fur.

I guess it might've seemed practical to get the picture of Max into my head as soon as that boy had entered the room. But, in truth, Max and this boy were very different. Their height differed, I'm pretty sure their age was not the same, and there was just nothing similar about them. But, the girl in front of me had the same height, almost the same color hair, and although she looked different, she still reminded me of Sarah. It was just her sudden appearance, nothing else. Or, maybe it was the fact that her smile, the way she walked reminded me of one of my favorite owners.

So, obviously, I began to lose myself in the thought of my Sarah standing before me. *Sarah right there. Sarah petting my fur. Sarah staring at me with her sweet, brown eyes and phone in one hand.*

But, the moment went away. Just like that, it vanished. My brain focused my eyes on the reality instead of any blooming fantasy. She wasn't Sarah. She was some other girl. And the way she placed her hands on my fur was something new I was experiencing. Sarah had her rough, but kind way of petting me. She always dug her warm skin in my fur and carried me up to her room. But, right now, I wasn't imagining her room. Instead, I was fixating my eyes on the dark yellow walls surrounding me, the big screen, and the large cushion I had sat on.

"Aww, Cody's here," the girl said as soon as she had crossed the threshold of the door. She automatically bent down, smoothly moving her hand across my fur.

"Yeah, Max and Sarah have gone to Alaska, and their mom dropped their dog before I got here," the other boy had said in response. Did I hear my owner's names? *No,* I tell myself. *Ignore it.*

"Paxton, can you turn that off now? How long have you been playing?" the girl said. And just like that, another foreign term entered my mind. *Paxton.* That must be the boy's name. The only mystery left to solve: what is the girl's name? What is the name of the girl who so deeply reminds me of Sarah? What is her real identity, so that I'm not hallucinating that Sarah is beside me?

To my luck, Paxton responds with her name. "Fine, Sandra. We can just play with Cody then." I didn't even care that I had heard my name come out of Paxton's whiny voice. Only one thing started circling through my mind. *Sandra. Sandra. Sandra.*

The name was so similar to Sarah's that I could picture her face again. Throw off Sandra's average face and replace it with Sarah's beautiful brown eyes and clean skin. Her wonderful clean scent, and her warm hands as she sat next to me on the sofa in our home.

And then my mom and my dad came through my mind.

Then Max. To be clear, I refer to Max and Sarah's parents as my own since they did adopt me, but in reality, they really aren't. Either way, this flush of memories was swarming through my mind before Paxton and Sandra clouded my vision and surrounded me. They each took turns petting me, and I probably could've described the hundred percent different feeling I was encountering right there.

***

I honestly couldn't tell what Paxton and Sarah were thinking, but I certainly knew my own feelings. Anger, sorrow, and just being left alone. I had wanted consolation but not anymore.

After Paxton and Sandra pet me a few times and talked with each other, it was the same cycle over again. Sandra turned on the big black screen and sounds exploded out of it.

I crawled back up onto the couch, and honestly, I kind of felt myself inching over to Sandra. But, I tried my best to stay where I was. The last thing that I wanted to happen was to go through the same flood of emotions.

To my luck, Sandra soon turned off the TV. And the first thing she did was stare at me, placing her calm hand onto my stiff body. She rocked her hands back and forth. I ignored her pats and just laid where I was. I guess now was the time when this loneliness hit me the worst. After all, I was surrounded by the two people who I didn't want to be with.

Suddenly, footsteps boomed onto the wooden floor.

Despite my exaggeration, the clickity sound of someone's shoes did make the whole room seem loud. I immediately lifted my head up towards the appearance of the mother.

"Can I give him a treat?" Sandra asked the mother.

"I already gave him one, but I think he can have one or two more," the woman replied.

And with their confusing conversation finished, Sandra headed towards my bag. My eyes darted to the treat box inside of it which she pulled out and stuck her hand into. Oh my gosh, I was getting another treat! And with not another second to waste, my legs carried me over to the pot of gold waiting over at the other end of the rainbow. It was a short ride. Their carpet didn't cover too much space.

As Sandra pulled out a treat and held it in her hand, Paxton soon rushed in. "Hey! I want to give him a treat," he said, starting to lunge for the treat box. I guess I'm getting more than one now.

My eyes locked onto each one of them, anticipation filling up inside me for who would set down the treat for me to gobble up. But, instead, they started a quarrel and their mother soon interjected.

"Hey, Sandra, you can give him his food later. Let Paxton give him a treat."

Sandra took a deep breath and replied with a "Fine." She handed the box of *gold* over to Paxton, and my legs could've just blasted off from right there. And I almost did. I jumped for it in his hand while he hid it behind his back with my tongue swirling around the inside of my mouth. What was going on? Were we playing "Fight for the Treat" or some other game?

"He keeps jumping for it," Paxton complains.

"Place it down for him to eat," Sandra replies.

"In the kitchen," the mother adds.

As my tongue tried to catch the treat in his small hands, he soon backed away and placed the treat on the kitchen floor. Exactly like the woman did. But honestly, it didn't matter. I leapt for it, just as my mouth grabbed the tiny piece. My strong teeth tore into it, and the wonderful taste overtook my mouth.

"Wow, he ate the whole thing in one bite," Paxton says, staring at me with amazement while I ignored his gaze.

Mhm, the treat was delicious. And, I was waiting for my second one. But, to my misfortune, there was no second one. So, with the remains of the treat causing a party in my mouth, I hurried over to the carpet where I could have the feeling of comfort and deliciousness combined. In the background, the family laughed at me, and I was left wondering why.

"Look, he took it to the carpet." one member said.

"Why is he doing that?" another asked.

"He must like the texture or something." They all ended with more giggles and laughs.

While they continued to share thoughts and laughs in

the living room, I remained where I was on the rug. Sandra and Paxton both came over to pet me. Their hands reached across my head, my body and even a slight touch on my nose. I licked Paxton's hand placed in front of my face as he began to giggle and talk to Sandra.

At this point, I was becoming itchy underneath. So, with my loyal *servants* by my side, I flipped over onto my back. "I think he wants a belly rub," Sandra said. She began to drag her nails onto the few hairs of my stomach at a fast pace. Every single spot that irritated me was soothed by her.

Paxton gave me a rub, too, but it was not as enjoyable. He didn't have any nails, and his hands surely did not meet my requirements of a satisfactory belly rub.

***

Seconds passed. It felt like hours. That is a typical thing to say, but it really felt like that. Being stuck in this frickin' simulation of my family led me to wait for hours and hours. I just wanted to leave because I couldn't handle any more of Sandra's belly rubs. I wanted belly rubs from Sarah. I wanted her to be touching my fur. I wanted her to be with me. But, sadly, she wasn't. Nor was Max. Nor was my mother. And nor was my father. They were all gone, and I was left waiting for their arrival if they ever did come back.

Now, it was lunch time. Instead of giving me another treat, Sandra took the initiative to provide food to me. She diligently took out a small box of meat and mixed it with rice into my food bowl. I took one stare at it and left. I wasn't hungry right then. And although the meat looked tempting, I wasn't just not in the mood. I didn't want Sandra to be giving me food. I wanted Sarah to. I wanted my mother to. I wanted one of them here with me, staring down at me with their smiles and lovely faces as they would dump the meat in the bowl.

I couldn't tell what Sandra was feeling there. I heard her muffled voice speak. "Cody isn't eating," but I honestly didn't care.

She constantly came up to me, lying on her belly or simply resting her back on the couch, and repeating my name several times. I could tell that she was trying to get me to eat my food with her cute charms. After a while, she dragged her body towards the food bowl and pointed at it. She even took my food bowl and dragged it towards me.

Pretty soon, I gave up. I gave up trying to think that they weren't my real family.

I crawled over to the bowl onto the ground and took a bite of food. It was delicious, and although I wasn't visually turned towards Sandra, I could picture the smile start to grow on her face. After all her attempts at getting me to eat, she must be smiling.

While I was eating, I heard footsteps slowly starting to fade. When I turned, there was nobody there. Yeah, I had been left alone all over again. But, I guess this was the one time when it seemed fine. This was the first time when I didn't feel a stream of tears leave my eyes. Of course, it reminded me of the way my parents had left me. How my family had left me. With just a wave of goodbye. Not a hug, not a pet, and not a word.

I walked into the wooden hallway, catching Sandra's leaving body hurtle a bag towards the stars. *Her leaving body. My mom's leaving body...*

I began to form those repeated actions in my head until all of a sudden, there appeared the person I'd been longing to see. Her pretty, thin brown hair, her pretty brown eyes, her clean skin, and her awkward smile gazing at me. Her eyes were targeting mine, and she was calling me up. Her backpack was hung over one shoulder and had the name "Sarah" sewn into it. My tiny legs were immediately compelled to follow her as I hopped up the steps, rushing to catch up to her.

In the distance, I heard Max's voice loud and clear. He was screaming at someone like he usually did. I had no idea what he did in his room the room doors closed most of the time. But, I followed Sarah all the way into her room. And, as soon as I came in, everything felt fresher, cooler, and spacious. And, the sunlight poured onto her bed. The walls had pink, vertical stripes painted all over it. Everything else was white.

I started to become disoriented. I don't understand: I never had this feeling in Sarah's room. Why was I feeling it now? Everything felt different, but Sarah's room was pretty tiny and full. Her curtains were usually pulled tight.

Sarah went straight to her desk, pulling out a folder with a bunch of papers. She grabbed a black stick pushing on one end and dragging it across the paper at the other end. And, I could suddenly remember this moment from many moments before. Sarah with her tasty "homework," a corner crumpled hanging off of the desk which I would then bite. Oh, her homework was delicious. I loved it. But, she didn't. She didn't love her homework, and she especially didn't love it when I bit it. I would always get a timeout when I took a small nibble from the corner.

Only now, there's something different. Now, her homework was perfectly straight, perfectly kept within the borders of the table, and her eyes were targeting it as she hurriedly moved her pencil across it. And, suddenly my eyes unveiled what I was trying to ignore. This wasn't Sarah's room; instead, it was Sandra's. I was still stuck inside their alien house, with a bunch of aliens themselves, constantly wondering how my family could leave me.

I hurried out of Sandra's room as she turned to look at me. I galloped towards the stairs and she followed. I could hear her footsteps so cleanly as she started to catch up to me. But, I hurried down the stairs before she could come and pet me again or offer consolation.

I turned to look up at the view from downstairs when I had arrived on the very first step. Paxton was out now, and both of them were staring at me. In the distance, I heard footsteps, probably of the mother, and behind me I heard the voice of the dad talking to someone with his doors still closed.

And, with the view of the family similar to mine, my mind reverted back to thinking about their pretty faces. Instead of reality. Sarah's short body, Max's tall body next to hers, my mom's visible body in the distance, and my dad's warm voice quietly speaking behind me. But, not everything can be changed to the way I want. The voices of the Johnson family overpowered those of my own Walter family. And, in my head, a confused voice asked: what is happening? What is happening to Max and Sarah? Why does my dad's voice sound different? Why does my mom look different?

So, with confusion boiling up in my head, my legs gave me a break by simply laying down on the comfy carpet located near the door, something definitely not in my house. But, it was good nonetheless. My eyes only had to focus on the wooden planks of the floor. Wait. No. This is making it worse. There are no wooden planks in my house, just tile. Yet another dose of disorientation for my brain.

I closed my eyes shut. Hopefully, this would help make everything better. In the background, I heard the family talking. And although I knew so deeply that it was the Johnsons, I was praying and praying that it might turn out to be the Walters — *my* family.

"What is happening to Cody?" Paxton asks.

"I don't know. He was fine before," Sandra responds.

"Mom, Cody's laying down by the door."

Now, I hear the louder footsteps of the mother. "Oh, he's probably waiting for the Walters," she replies. I heard my last name be spoken, but I ignored it. I just needed a moment to myself.

"Is he still sad over them leaving? Haven't they left him before?" Sandra asked.

"I don't know. It must be different now. He's not used to this place. It will take him a while," the mother answers.

"Should we leave him alone?" Paxton asks.

"Let's sit with him," Sandra says. "I'm bored anyways."

With those words leaving her mouth, I heard her crouch down beside me on her two legs, reaching to pet me. I felt a nice drag of her hand across my fur, but I didn't flinch. She gave me a pat on my head and moved her arm across my back. Her face moved in closer with my body, and I could smell her scent. It overpowered the faded scent of my departed mother. But, she quickly jerked her head back. I had no idea why. I was starting to enjoy her smell and her existence near me. It kind of reminded me of Sarah. No, what am I saying? She was not Sarah and she never will be.

Sandra comes over to my front side, trying to catch my gaze. And, although my eyes aren't directed exactly towards hers, I catch the dark brown iris in her eye, the bright reflection on the side, and the white part of her eyeball glowing.

She began to speak, "Hi, Cody. You're so cute, aren't

you? Are you bored or simply sad? Are you waiting for the Walters to come back?" I heard my family's name again, but for some reason, I didn't revert to thinking about them or get teary-eyed. She spoke again. "We can keep you company, Cody. We can hang out with you. Just for a few days before they come back. So, can you get up now? Spend some time with us? I know you don't understand me, but I'm hoping right now — I'm wishing," she said.

I honestly had no idea what she was saying, but right then and there, I felt something. It wasn't sadness, it wasn't loneliness, it was love. It was a red heart exiting Sandra's face coming towards my teary eyes. And, suddenly, I realized, this family wasn't replacing mine. They were simply taking care of me, comforting me, looking after me while my family were enjoying themselves. And, although it hurts to know that they are enjoying themselves without me, there must have been a rational explanation to why I wasn't allowed to tag along. For the time being, I have to make peace with them leaving. Afterall, this isn't going to be my permanent home. It's just temporary. It's just a temporary place where I have to spend a few days, getting to know a whole other caring family.

With a vial of sadness still taking up a piece of my heart, I got up and into Sandra's now open lap. She looked startled, but then pet me across the back. Paxton joined in, too. The mother came, holding an apple in her hand, and I leapt for it. With so many complex emotions overwhelming me, I needed a snack. Plus, they already had that gray rectangular apple in their midst.

This was the moment where I finally met the dad. He left the room, came over and pet me as I soon gave up jumping for the apple in the mother's hand. I hadn't really interacted with him much, so I was glad to be able to see his face and tall body. As he approached me, I let him pet my body, but then I needed a belly rub. He stiffened his fingers and scratched my stomach. Sandra joined in, too, and the two of them rubbed their nails across my belly, relieving me. Aah, so nice. I had been waiting for a time like this.

***

The next few days were spent creating wonderful memories. I hid under the Johnson's comfy bed, which reminded me of the shelter where I had spent a lot of my childhood, hid under their sofa, and sunbathed outside. On walks, I would mark my territories where I couldn't pick up any other dog's scent. The Johnsons always laughed when I did this, referring to it as "peeing" or whatever that meant. But, I always trotted along, pulling them with me.

Although there were a few moments where I wanted to run back to my family and forget this place even existed, I brushed off any sadness trying to flood my mind and focused on the happiness I was feeling right here. Because, I had another home. I had another place where I could explore love, comfort, and enjoyment.

Well, it was until my family came back and took me home with them. All of a sudden, the memory of this house started to wash away. I was there, in my family's arms, on the soft carpet, and the low couch. But, I knew that somewhere, deep inside my brain, memories of this experience would remain. They had to. It was my *other home*. It was another home from the one I already had. Another lovely home. That's right, it was a home, not merely just a place of residence, but somewhere that nurtures the feeling of family.

Influenced

Clara:

Another day, another seven hours of school. And another 420 minutes where I couldn't shine my best because of the others. All because of lack of effort, care, and disaffection that the other kids' showed towards everything in school besides lunch. Nerds weren't appreciated at our school — by teachers, yes, but not by other students — try-hards were shamed upon, and now, you'll see people trying less. Getting worse graders, flunking tests, getting into mischief, and not paying attention in class.

Just like everyone else, I have never liked school. How could I? I'd rather curl up at home in my bed watching movies and TV shows all day long instead of using my brain to answer countless questions, but there's one thing that very few people, including me, know about being able to go to school. It is important. It's a gift and we should be lucky to receive it. Yes, it's tiring, and yes it may seem boring and maybe useless or even tedious, but it's the foundation for everything in the future.

I wished, desperately wished, that everything was different. That more people started to care, that people wouldn't have to hide their brains to look cool. But, all I can do is wish, wish, wish. It's not like any of this will ever come true. The kids will continue to be rebellious and lazily spend the rest of their lives doing nothing useful.

Kelli:

My alarm's shrieking vibrations entered my ears. It was a complete disaster of sounds for a singer like me. With my eyes still closed shut, my hand reached to click the snooze button on my iPhone. But, of course, I just had to hit the Stop button. So, after I noticed a few minutes later that my alarm wasn't snoozing for nine more minutes, I reluctantly stomped out of bed and went to my bathroom. It was a Monday. School time. Stupid school time. A stupid seven hours of my life wasted.

Honestly, why do we even need school? It's just a bunch of useless facts that are dumped into my brain and then soon forgotten. History doesn't seem to be benefiting me at all, we have calculators to do math for us, and what do I care about how the Earth works with its scientific explanations? Lastly, I don't think English is necessary at this age. I think I'm familiar with English now, and I certainly don't need to spend any longer identifying parts of speech and metaphors.

Would someone just show me why, until this present day, us kids are forced to sit through long classes of useless torture? I wasn't against dressing up nicely and meeting my friends, but I continuously wish that I didn't have to waste my time while doing so. I just wish, desperately wish, that everything was different. That maybe we'll be spared, that perhaps school can at least be shortened and become easier or maybe I'll find the reason why school exists. But, all I can do is wish, wish, wish. It's not like any of this will ever come true.

Clara:

When I got up this morning, it was cloudy outside. After washing my face, everything became slightly blurry. It wasn't like I couldn't see anything, but more like there was something wrong, something twisted, something not exactly real about everything.

I had eggs — a nice, healthy breakfast for my brain — before grabbing all my supplies and heading out of the door. My mom shuffled behind me, car keys in her hand and her bag in another. She hurried inside our car and started it; we pulled out of the driveway.

I arrived at school after a few minutes and climbed out. As I hurried across the sidewalk to the school's side entrance, I saw the countless number of kids with their musical instrument in one hand, and a phone in the other, their eyes entranced by the tiny screen. I kept my phone safe in my backpack and would take it out later. Many also had Airpods on or those huge Beats headphones stuck to their ears as others just stared at the oncoming door. But, there was one thing each student was doing: stopping at the view of a sign on the door. When I approached it, it read *The Brain Contest! May the best brain win!*

As everyone, including me, stared dumbfounded at the poster, we soon scrambled inside to see a man on the stage. He had a peculiar outfit on: a black shirt with pants, and a black hat. I was receiving a mysterious vibe from him. I think some of the others could perceive that, too as he remained on the stage, staring at us fish with his half dolphin, half shark eyes.

Kelli:

As soon as I had passed the threshold of my front door, the gray skies first caught my attention. Usually, it's sunny where we live, but I guess the skies had simply copied my own feelings and shown them through its huge, dark clouds.

I caught the bus and found my friends in the back seats, chatting with the boys next to us. I forced a smile on my face and rolled out my shoulders before joining them in the back. "Hello, peoples, Kelli is here." I stated, arousing attention for my friends in the back.

They smiled at me. One replied, "Hey, Kelli, we were just chatting about this new trend and the upcoming cheer tryouts. You are doing it, right?"

"Yeah of course," I replied.

With the limited chatter in the bus, the occasional whispers, and mostly blank expressions staring out of the window, you could likely hear our gossip from miles. Our pretty voices filled the bus as we talked about this new trend we found on social media and the plan to go to the mall this weekend. "We can go for laser tag and then maybe Sephora. I really need some new mascara," my friend said.

The rest of the bus ride was a relaxing eight minutes before we had to get off and into the disgusting crowd of instrument hoarders and ridiculous nerds. My friends and I hurried inside the school when the sign everybody was staring at caught our eyes. And, the dumbest thing was written on it.

"Brain contest? That's the stupidest thing I've heard. Who names a contest the brain contest? It must be some lame math thing. Whatever," my friend said.

I rolled my eyes at the words written to the poster as I led my friends inside where a man was on stage with a mic in one hand and a black magic hat in another. He was about to speak before we hurried to get a seat; I took out my phone from my pocket and ignored the man's weird and mysterious aura as I caught that try-hard Clara looking at me.

Clara:

"May I have everyone's attention please?" the man asked politely through the microphone. I was listening to his words, but more focused on what the populars were doing in the back. The girl, Kelli, mainly. She couldn't even put her phone down for a second and listen. Do they seriously think they are superior to everyone else? Judging by their smug expressions and disregard for paying attention, I'd say that's exactly what they thought of themselves.

The man tapped his mic again and the girls in the back rolled their eyes as they shared comments with the boys next to them. It wasn't until the man said, "Girls, please," on the mic that Kelli and her friends finally realized they should've been paying attention to the weirdo on stage.

The man started talking. "You obviously don't know who I am, and well, I might seem uncanny or mysterious to most of you, but that is okay." The girls and most of the boys grimaced at his words. I was impressed at how the man managed to read the expressions of so many different teenagers. Teenage years are a unique stage for human beings.

The man continued, "So, the reason I am here today is to cause a change. To influence you all. And, I promise, by the end, you will be influenced. So much so that I am known as the Influencer."

Kelli:

Is this man psycho or something? What is he saying? He is some influencer? I have never heard of him on Instagram before; he must not be a popular one. So, as his crowd let out murmurs about his words, I couldn't help but think smugly *we'll see, so-called influencer. We'll see.*

He moved his eyes across the cafeteria, focusing his

eyes with each of the students to get their attention back to him. As he faced us girls in the back, I had a sudden feeling that he was focusing on me. Me, more than anyone else. His green eyes locked into my blue eyes and he grinned. Maybe it was because I was rude in the beginning, but it felt like something a lot more. A token from the universe. A gift for me. Or a sliver of light in an area where I only see dark. Is he trying to influence me? To change me? No, this all sounds ridiculous; I can't believe I am considering or even worse — thinking all of this.

He continued on, "Now, there's diversity at this school. People who are good at sports, people are good at math and science, writers, artists, populars — he gave my friends and I a look — and pranksters. My favorites are people who put in effort in everything they do, try-hards, you might call them."

What exactly was he trying to say? Why would anyone in their right mind put effort into school? Just try a little, don't fail, and it's all good.

"Now, populars. I'm guessing you guys aren't nerds or don't think you have a lot of potential with math and using your brain for complex problems, but that's okay because you do. And you only find that potential when you actually realize the importance of it and train your brain to get better."

Clara:

Did I hear this man right? Honestly, I am not even sure since his words were a bit confusing, but my brain has pounced specifically on the words "importance, brain, and influence." Suddenly, I had elapsed into this whole other reality where others might start to care. About school and effort. But, it soon faded because the whole scenario was unbelievable.

I wasn't even sure what this man's true intentions were. He might've just been a hoax; after all, I have never heard of somebody called the Influencer who wears a black magic hat and black attire, talking about different types of teenagers and wanting to change their minds. Maybe, this is all just a dream. A good dream in a sense. And, now, let's continue it.

The man spoke again, "I'm guessing all of you saw the sign out there about a Brain Contest. I get it, a totally lame name. Honestly, it should just be called the Contest because it's more then using the math and science side of the brain. There will be multiple mini contests in this competition, and a grand prize will be given out.

Possibly lacking any attention and having a half-asleep expression towards the man's words, I'm pretty sure everyone's eyes lit up at the sound of the grand prize. The populars in the back stared at one another with a confident look on their faces and began to whisper in each others' ears. I was thrilled, too; more thrilled about what could be the result, according to the man. But, obviously, he was crazy for thinking that he'd be able to change a whole group of teenagers' minds. I wonder what was the rationale for the teachers to invite him. Surely, they must've had some skepticism. How can they believe he can make such a huge difference, especially through a contest?

When faced with competition and a grand prize on the line, teenagers' eyes turn red with fire and their arms become stiff. Their opponent will shiver in fear or fight back and appear tough. And, the next thing you know, there are two teenagers clamoring at each other and shouting out accusations of cheating, or fighting almost to the point of death. Well, that's exaggerated, but sometimes it's scary. I personally think he should've kept the grand prize a secret.

Kelli:

We've got this. I've got this. Yes, my brain and math skills may not be as strong as the few nerds competing, but I am popular, I am pretty, and I can surely use my skills of persuasion and compulsion. I will take home the grand prize, that I am sure of.

As I was lost in my own world with the grand prize, the Influencer took a section of all the kids in the cafeteria, specifically the students in the back, and separated them into two equal groups. My friends and I, the boys we were talking to, and a few other lame students were separated. He pulled a white board in front of us and quickly scribbled something on it. An equation. A stupid math equation. And the nerds were on the other side of the cafeteria. I honestly felt like I was by myself on this one since the man was staring straight at me. His pupils fixated on my constantly moving eyes, trying to avoid his gaze. He moved his pupils at the last second, but he had given me a good stare. It wasn't intimidating, rather more encouraging as if he saw some potential in me. It was kind and almost altruistic, like he knew something about me and wanted to help.

I must've been overthinking it, so I shook it off as the Influencer started speaking. "What is this equation used for?"

He looked at my team as most of us avoided looking at him. After a few seconds, he stared at the other team. "Anyone?" he asked.

I looked up at the equation he had written on the board in his huge, but neat font. I felt a sense of familiarity, and I recognized the equation. I may not have been the smartest, but even the dumbest person could've told what the equation was for. So, with beaming confidence, I simply answered, "Speed." It wasn't too loud, and it wasn't too quiet, so even though the Influencer was facing the other team, he heard my response. And he smiled. He beamed. I think there was a flicker in his eyes.

"Correct," he said. My friends behind me gave me a low high five, whispering *good job* in my ear. "It was an easy equation but being able to answer in front of the whole grade takes confidence."

I looked away from his eyes, and I couldn't help but smile. Yes, it was scary even though I was popular. And, yet, I had still done it. Someone had to, and I wanted to win the grand prize, so it had to be me.

Clara:

That girl Kelli thinks too highly of herself. She may be popular, she may be talented at everything besides facts and tests, and she may be speaking in front of the entire grade, but I know what she is doing isn't terrifying. It can't be like that for a simple science equation. So, as I caught her smiling with the Influencer turned away, I couldn't help but roll my eyes. Unfortunately, the Influencer had me here, in the middle of all of these jocks, nerds, and others, just having to desperately wait for my chance to answer. He separated us for a reason. He wanted the dumb populars to answer the question, and make them feel good about themselves since we all know one thing they can't do is math. Yeah, well, I say, they shouldn't be feeling good about themselves. They didn't accomplish such a big feat.

"Now, why do we need speed? Why do we need this formula?" He stared at Kelli again. I scrunched my eyebrows in frustration. Can't he ask us, too?

"I'm sorry, what?" Kelli asked.

"I asked, why do we need speed?" His voice was surprisingly calm and patient. It seemed like he had all day. I know only a few minutes had passed, but at this rate, the competition would never finish. All I could do was wonder if school was even going to happen.

"To calculate the speed of things," Kelli's friend answers.

"But what things?" He gave Kelli's group a long stare before turning to the other team. "You guys have an idea?" They all desperately shook their heads. "Can you guys guess? It's alright if you are wrong."

Some boy took a gulp before answering, "Race cars, Ferraris, sonic jets, running."

"Yes, thank you," the Influencer said, "it was a pretty simple answer. There are lots of things, objects, and even animals that have speed. But, my question is, why do we need it?" He turned back to the other group as the room was shredded in silence. Students either stared blankly, thought about the answer, or pretended to think by facing another way and looking up at the ceiling. "Kelli, do you know?" The sound of her name from a complete stranger created murmurs throughout the cafeteria. Kelli herself was shocked beyond a point where it couldn't be described. From looking down and avoiding the Influencer's gaze, she looked straight into his eyes as he smiled back. Something fishy was going on: Kelli had never told her name out loud.

Kelli:

Is this person a stalker? Knowing my name without me telling it seems fishy to me. I should have known. After all, his smile is kind yet creepy at the same time, he keeps staring at me, and he's interested in what I've got to say. I doubt he is some angel or god sent from above, so a stalker is what I conclude.

I was ready to punch him in the face. Stalking a teenage girl? I was about to glare at him as he spoke, "Now, Kelli, your friends are just very loud. I overheard your name." His voice was so calm, like the movement of water in a small stream. His face didn't show signs of some creepy dude who was a stalker. Instead, I was facing a man with a kind face. It was difficult to remain angry, and he had a point. We were loud.

"So, Kelli, do you know the answer?"

Right. I'm supposed to answer. Would it be okay to say I don't know? I'm guessing that's what is expected of me in front of this crowd. "Um, to help, no sorry, to give us the speed, so we know it." I stammered as I spat something random out. I was completely stuck.

But the man didn't call on anyone else. Instead he said, "Wow, that's very close. Can you elaborate?"

"Um, um." I stammered again, not really sure what else

to say. What was this man looking for? I desperately stared at the crowd, at the jocks, the nerds, and the thousands of kids staring at me as my cheeks blushed from embarrassment and my eyes tried to avoid the man's gaze. I caught that know-it-all girl Clara staring at me intently. I could bet that she knew the answer right about now. I bet she wanted to answer. In fact, with my brain not responding, I desperately hoped that she would answer. Or anyone for that matter. The silence is scaring me, and I feel humiliated being the center of attention. The center of attention who had to answer the question that probably had a million answers but one that I could not find. Stupid school. I wish I never came today. Maybe I could've just called in sick. Gone out to eat or go to the mall or something instead of wasting my hours here, only hearing the crickets outside and the air conditioning making quiet sounds from its fan.

I desperately hoped that someone might end this silence.

Clara:

This is killing me. I have the urge to yell out the answer right in front of everyone as I stare at Kelli's pink cheeks and nervous glances. I have the urge to end this awkward silence and hear my voice instead of the air conditioning's annoying squeaks.

And, I couldn't hold it in any longer. I shouted out what

I hoped was what the Influencer was looking for, "To give us the knowledge about how fast something can travel in a specific time. It's quite necessary because knowledge is what creates the world we live in. Without it, we'd have nothing and we'd be nothing. Knowledge and intelligence is what drives humans, and quite literally, speed drives us." I smiled at the end as everyone's faces were on me. But, I didn't once blush, and I didn't look away. I had wanted to do this for so long, and I finally got the chance to shine like I wanted to. It seemed like the Influencer's face was also shining.

"Wow, wonderful. Absolutely extraordinary. You are so right, Ms. — "

"Clara," I answered.

"Clara." As he said that, his mouth just seemed trained by the phonics of my name. I almost felt that he had said my name before, or at least knew it. No, it was more like he knew *me*. In the world of strangers, in the world of so many unknown humans, I didn't know him but he knew me. And, he was just waiting for me to blurt out the answer.

The Influencer spoke, "You know, I wanted dear Kelli here to try to answer, but that was an amazing answer, Clara. I hope you all were listening to her; she spoke amazingly. And, she's totally right. Knowledge is the key to everything. More than just knowledge about math equations — he pointed to the equation on the white board — more than just facts, knowledge about anything and everything it what builds our lives and the future."

All I could do was beam. I was finally getting recognition from a new person. Not from a teacher, not from my parents, not from a sarcastic student, but an absolute stranger who actually appreciated my opinions and thoughts. At this moment, I felt the sun shining down on me through the ceiling or maybe a nearby window. I felt the air conditioner whistling a pretty tune, and I imagined that all the students in the cafeteria were murmuring my name in victory. But, the moment went away. Right after the Influencer moved from this topic and I was left feeling like nothing again.

I could see the bright reflection in some students' eyes as they seemed to be taking into consideration what I said, but the majority of the students looked like zombies, staring at the Influencer with blank expressions and sulking and groaning as the Influencer started to speak about the next few competitions. I even heard a student shout out, "Dude! Just give us the prize! Or is there even one? I wouldn't be surprised if you're just tricking us all!" But, the Influencer remained completely unfazed, resuming his talk about the next competition. I listened, imagining the moment where I'd save the day again.

Kelli:

I guess I shouldn't have doubted Clara. She was always saving everyone's back in class, yelling out answers as the teachers would be grilling students who couldn't do anything but innocently beg for mercy, claiming that they didn't know, that the question was too confusing, that they didn't understand, and a whole lot of other crap.

"Okay, so this next competition will be all about computers. I'm pretty sure everybody here enjoys computers. They're life-saving, convenient, extraordinary, but how exactly are they made? How are they set up? How do they just function the way they do? Some of those questions will be left unanswered by this competition, but you might get a better idea about these special machines."

I focused on what the Influencer said this time. I didn't dare daydream about something else. I had to be ready, in case I was the victim again. But, I was desperately hoping not. I couldn't face that attention again, so many eyes staring at me to give an answer I had no idea how to answer.

I heard the Influencer explain that a computer screen has tiny squares called pixels. All I could do was nod my head *of course.* I may not have been the star of math, but I had basic knowledge like this. He went on talking about the parts of a computer: the RAM, the Motherboard, the CPU. But much more important than any part of the computer is how it is able to store tons of information in its memory and take the instructions from code to create gazillion websites and features.

Apparently, this next competition, while pretty straightforward, was meant to imitate how a computer functions in the simplest way. All I could do was grimace as the Influencer explained this competition. After the last round, I glued my hands together and prayed. Luckily, there were teams, so maybe I wouldn't have to be the one to suffer the most.

Clara:

"The whole cafeteria is a pixel maze. There will be 6 teams, each has a starting point in different corners of the cafeteria." Suddenly, it was like magical dust had created a pixel mat on the floor, cleared out the numerous tables and chairs, and set up each of the starting points with two computers each. One second, we were standing in a plain, simple cafeteria; the next, we were standing in some amazing, unknown room with an outstanding carpet and remarkable computers.

"There's more to a computer than this challenge will bring. However, each team will answer questions on a computer to help build a computer. Ironic, isn't it? There's a total of three computers. One that provides a question, one that gives information on how to assemble and code computers, and the last one which you will assemble.

"When you answer a question correctly, one of you will move three steps forward on the pixel mat. At different points, there will be a computer part which someone will take back to your team's base and attach it together. Don't worry, you have everything to help you and your own common sense. Then, someone will enter the code that is given to you. By the end, you'll have created a rookie computer. Trust me, it's not as hard as you think. Whoever builds their computer first wins!"

Okay, enough talking. I need to begin; I will lead my team to victory again. By the end of this, I won't be surprised if I win the grand prize. Who knows, maybe I'll receive a check of a million dollars or maybe something more reasonable like a thousand dollars. Either way, that's a lot of money.

My heart rate was starting to speed up and I felt my body wiggling. Not an ounce of nervousness filled me; instead, I was having excitations. My body could practically jump up and down like a little kid again, simply attracted to the feeling of getting ice cream or a toy.

"Now, make sure you are *all* contributing and collaborating," the Influencer added.

"What the heck does "collaborating" mean?" some dumb kid yelled through the crowd, laughing. A boy next to him bonked him in the head, replying, "It means to work together, doofus."

The whole cafeteria had laughed in response, yelling out names, but the Influencer seemed preoccupied or more of just unfazed, again. He didn't care what that kid had said, nor cared what the thousands of kids were yelling at him. He was a strange man.

But, what was even stranger was how he was able to equally split us all apart. All the nerds, all the bullies, all the populars, all the extras mixed in equally, so that each team had a smart student and a couple of dumb. So peculiar. And so mysterious.

Kelli:

I do not like my group. No friends, just a bunch of freaks staring at me. I don't know if they were expecting me to provide help, or staring at me like I was some extra student who had no right to be in their group.

I smiled awkwardly, turning away as some boy in our group turned towards the question that had popped up on the computer. All I thought about was whether these questions would all involve math and science. Luckily, they weren't. There were countless questions that were basic common sense, probably made so that anyone could answer them.

I could say, in fact, that I answered a lot of them. I was surprised when a few questions came up about how to apply makeup and what ingredients to put into a cake. Strange. Very odd. If the Influencer came up with these questions, I guess it should have been expected since he's the icon of being mysteriously unusual.

Within seconds, I pretty much became the leader of my team. From staring awkwardly as the nerd on our team scrambled to answer the first two questions and wait for someone to walk onto the pixel mat, I took a deep breath and initiated everything. I took over the computer with the questions and had one of the nerd focus on assembling the computer and programming it. The rest was with me, answering any of the difficult questions, which I always dreaded. Then, someone volunteered to be the one to walk on the pixel mat, and that was their job. One of the larger boys could handle weight, so he was assigned to pick up the computer parts and put them together with the nerd's instructions. The other person, as much as I wanted to say was helping out, didn't have such a major role. She helped us for a few questions, stared at the other teams, and made sure every teammate was contributing, which was ironic given that she was contributing nothing.

As easy as this all might've sounded, creating these different roles for everyone was beyond easy. We argued a lot in the beginning over why I was the one leading everyone as if it wasn't already expected. We also learned the hard way that phones weren't allowed. I took out my phone for a question, and before I could even unlock it, it was no longer in my hand. It had vanished, gone like some magician had sprinkled magic powder over it. It was the strangest thing ever. I'm just glad that everyone's phones had vanished before they could've started using them.

Clara:

Moments passed. Countless questions were answered. My group was one of the easiest to work with, surprisingly. Everyone did something and found their place. I had a popular on my team and she volunteered to be the one to stand on the pixel mat.

Within minutes, we were at a good place, staring at all the other team's nervous faces. Some were just staring at each other in complete silence and zero movements. But, we led our team to victory. I answered a lot of the questions; I had someone from the team help me assemble and lift the computer parts.

We heard the Influencer's bright and hyper voice as soon as we had finished entering the code for the computer. He blew a huge horn that caught everyone's attention, and then with everything blurred and I feeling disoriented, the computers disappeared, the pixel mat vanished, and in its place was the same, boring cafeteria I have been staring at for the past two years.

"Congratulations, Clara's team, Team 6, for winning this competition! Before we go into the next one, let's discuss what we learned from this one." Before anyone could say anything, everyone stared dumbfounded at what the cafeteria had turned into. There were puzzled expressions on everyone's faces, but no one questioned anything out loud.

Instead, we sped straight into a discussion. The Influencer asked everyone how their mindsets had changed during this competition and exactly why he might've hosted it. Before I could answer, someone else did. And her answer was perfect. She had finally realized how important it is to put effort into what she did, to understand just a little bit of something we use so much in life, to pay attention to the knowledge that mattered. I beamed. As much as it hurt that I couldn't have earned recognition for saying that, at least someone else did. Lots of other students added other little tidbits before we rolled into the next competition and the few more after that. Trivia, running, diy's, and so many others. Groans were heard from every student, and soon the whole school day was taken away.

Little did I know that they weren't all about math and science and knowledge. Some were simply about talent.

Kelli:

Finally, just finally, after exhausting my brain and body on so many factual questions and competitions, I was thrilled to take a break and do what I did best. Sing. Let my voice take control. The very last contest was like a talent show. The three most exquisite, the most unique talents would be awarded either first, second, or third place.

So many faces drenched in fear, others drowned in

arrogance, but I remained confident. I was an amazing singer, and I could finally show that. Rid people's minds of that scene earlier with me staring dumbfounded at the math equation. Eventually create a whole new impression.

"Being smart, having knowledge, being able to think and pick up on topics quickly isn't the only thing that will help you in life. So is giving effort in everything you do. Without effort, without a care, how will anything get done?

"For this next challenge, we are showcasing talents. Talents are tricky things. While they may seem natural, I know that you definitely need practice, effort, and passion to keep them alive. All of you must have some talent, whether little or small. And, if you don't, then, today is the day to try something new. Put some effort into something you aren't good at so that you can have a better mindset and have a chance of winning my grand prize.

"Okay, so you have 40 minutes to prepare and then 5 minutes max to showcase it. This will give all the artists, both in music and with drawings, time to practice and actually take time to draw what you will showcase including anybody else who will need plenty of time to get ready for their talent."

My hands were shaking and my mouth just wanted to sing right then and there. I finally felt free when the Influencer stopped talking and let us run throughout the school to get ready for our talents. I hurried to the choir room, leaving my friends so that I could practice in private. Actually let my voice run free for a little while in the spacious room, feeling the sun on my face and my voice ringing in the cool air.

Clara:

Lucky for me that I am a talented individual. I have had many talents and skills come and go through the years. I have been able to create such realistic objects with colored pencils or paint, I know how to play the clarinet, and so many other talents from bending my thumb to being able to efficiently untie a knot. 40 minutes later, I had everything situated. I prepared my talent, executed it in time, and left with a smile on the Influencer's face. "Wow, that's a unique talent, Clara. Art with a science sense to it."

This talent show was probably the best that I have ever seen. Somehow, some way, each student in my middle school actually spent time nurturing their talent, preparing it, and thinking creatively on how to demonstrate it. Yes, of course, there were a few hiccups from some students, but it was an amazing sight to behold. I have never realized all the skills all my friends have. I caught my friends on the stage, dancing, expressing the cool tricks they could do, having fun which I have honestly never seen them do. I finally got the chance to chat with them after their turns.

Apparently, the populars teamed up. I had no idea that was allowed, but they pulled off a breathtaking performance led by Kelli. I had no idea that her singing was so passionate, so soothing, and fantastic. She sang as if this was her last time to sing while her friends used their hip-hop and cheer knowledge to dance. One of her friends apparently also knew how to play the piano, and out of nowhere, it showed up on the stage, ready for her use.

Lot of the popular boys, as expected, show off their sport-skills. They made plenty of trick shots, did tricks with a softball, played a game with a football, and even pulled off a surprising performance with a guitar.

The Influencer clapped after each one, and the smile on his face never diminished, nor did the smile on so many of the kids' faces. For this moment, it felt like we were all a bunch of first graders again instead of eighth graders, smiling at whatever good thing would happen to us, and exploring the world.

Kelli:

I think everyone was fascinated by my performance. I felt reassured since I had finally changed the minds of everyone here. And my own mind had been changed, too.

It's sad. I really enjoyed this challenge; I enjoyed them, all, really. It was a different sight to behold with everyone working so diligently to showcase their talents, and all us teenagers actually caring about what we put in for all the competitions before this one.

I was going to miss this. After all, this would never remain. Pretty soon, it would be over. The Influencer would give his grand prize to a student, and leave the rest of us while we chased that student for eternity, hoping to snatch the prize for ourselves. It was a good motivation for all of us, just not a good result.

"So, who gets the prizes?" a student walked up to the Influencer and asked.

"Oh, that. Well, that's too hard to decide. All of you had such unique skills, and most of you put in so much work. I think the school's hallways were silent with your concentration. So, I'm not really sure I could give an award to only three people. Everyone deserves it."

"Okay, nevermind that. Who gets the grand prize? What is your grand prize?"

"Well, all of you got that. And, now you're rich."

Everyone's eyes lit up, including mine. I don't know how this guy gave money to each of us, but the sound of wealth caught my eyes.

"How much money?" someone asked.

"Oh, no, not money." Everyone looked puzzled. "Your brains. Now, they're rich in math and quick thinking. They have a better mindset which will help you down the road. And, it will even help you focus to become rich. So, yeah, I gave you the foundation of life."

"You tricked us!" a student shouted.

"Yeah, you tricked us!" "How dare you!" "You're a fraud!" so many students yelled. I couldn't help but be angry, too, but because of the Influencer's words, I couldn't yell or shriek.

"Now, now, I understand, you feel that you have been betrayed, and I get that. I guess I probably should've given you guys something interesting. So, I'll give you something —"

"What?" everyone asked.

"The chance to watch me disappear." And with that said, he took out something from his pocket, threw at the floor, and with smoke billowing around his body, he was no longer there nor his white boards, equipment, and warm smile.

Clara:

That was when I woke up. The Influencer left, and I woke up with a jerk. I was in my bed, two minutes before my alarm clock rang.

I rubbed my eyes and turned my alarm off, disappointedly brushing my teeth and eating breakfast. Within minutes, I was dragging myself out the door, sulking at what a Monday would bring. A bunch of lazy, care-free teenagers. It would be a nightmare.

When I got to school, it was all a normal sight. The cafeteria tables aligned correctly, so many children on their phones or goofing around, but then I noticed something. Along with the goofiness, along with the chatter, many students were talking about school or had their homework out.

This intrigued me; homework was never out during this time. Usually, it was just 20 minutes on phones.

"Clara?" I turned to see the popular girl, Kelli facing me.

"Uh, hi," I answered.

"It was interesting, wasn't it?"

"What was?" I asked, completely confused.

"Never mind that. Did you know we have a new principal?"

"What? Really? Where did our other one go?"

"No idea, but you should see our new principal. His name is Mr. Neuer. He says he's going to change us all," Kelli said. I grimaced at the thought. I don't think he's going to change a bunch of teenagers.

"Yeah, he's going to influence so many teens? I don't think so."

"No, I think he already influenced us. After all, the Influencer sure left us all in an interesting state of mind."

That was the moment when I realized what I had dreamt was not a dream, but reality. And, now it was going to go one step further.

The Same

Sweet Home

A Sequel to Another, Lovely Home

The stars in the dark, evening sky twinkled from my window as my dad screeched our car to a halt – well, not with the sound since it was a luxurious car – in front of a house, likely larger than ours. Sarah climbed out, and following her actions, I trailed her and the bag she was carrying. The breeze was chilly outside; I could feel the wind airbrush my tight curls. I continued to follow Sarah with the rest of my family through the short grass in this dark atmosphere. The house there was glowing a golden color when we approached the steps leading up to the door, and something tingled inside of me that I think was a memory.

Sarah stared down at me just as my father hit his fist on the door. I stared back at her, just wanting to ask: *why are we here? What is in those bags? Are you staying with me?* Afterall, they had left me in the past.

As the bags Sarah was handling started to drag onto the brick surface of the doorway, I took a sniff. The bag smelled familiar. Very familiar. So, were the contents familiar then? But, the front door of the house opened before I could investigate what was inside.

When we walked in, four strangers were crowded at the door. To me, they really didn't look familiar, let alone smell familiar. But, then again, I was getting some sort of vibe from the golden light I saw earlier. I had definitely seen that before.

Either way, the owners of the house (the strangers according to me) started to hug my parents along with Sarah and Max. Upon seeing this, my mouth opened to bark. The family didn't look so startled, and turned their attention to me. I approached each of them, jumping onto their knees and sniffing their bodies. Every one of them — the girl and the two parents — extended their hands towards me and said my name when I jumped onto their knees except the last one. A boy. And, he was smelly. I don't know why, but suddenly some memory zapped through my brain about a boy like this one in front of me.

Before I could place my mind on this, my father started speaking, "I brought all of Cody's stuff: his food, treats, leash, toys, and a sweater to keep him warm." I was not sure why, but the family sure seemed fascinated by the sweater which looked so much like mine and started chatting with my family in their confusing language.

And then, the moment came where I didn't get hurt, but felt like I was bruised and at a loss of barks. Sarah picked me up in her arms and whispered the word "goodbye" in my ears before I was exchanged into the other woman's hands. And then, they were gone. They disappeared from my eyes. I could sense their scent fading from the door, and I could hear this harsh sound of their footsteps crawling into the car. I heard the car doors completely closing as they whooshed away from the house where they had left me. To make it all worse, I had witnessed my family leave me all over again. Leave me either with human strangers or large dogs whom I had no interest staying with.

As my gaze didn't leave the door where I had last seen my family, the woman who was carrying me gave me a rough pat. I immediately turned to her arm, sniffing it and receiving this nice, fragrant smell. After her, the only teenage girl in the house — so similar to my owner Sarah — gave me a stroke. I caught her scent, and she smelled interesting. It wasn't pleasant like the woman's, but something different; it was enough to lure me around her home. After the woman dropped me, the girl went all around the house: through the main hallway, through a couple of rooms, and up the stairs — with me tailing behind her. It was a lot more movement than I was used to, but what can I do? My legs simply listened to my nose.

Pretty soon, the girl hurried into a room with yellow light, closing the door behind her. I simply sat near the threshold. I can wait; it's fine. I'm sure she'll exit that room soon.

***

The girl finally came out. Her hair had vanished and instead this weird cloth was tied to the top of her head. The room behind her smelled of something that Sarah had forced me to use when I was prisoned in a bath of cruel water. She claimed it made me smell better, but the experience was awful. And, smelling this from the room, the girl reminded me of Sarah. The loneliness without my family was creeping back into me. I didn't want to be reminded of my family's leaving right now. And, either way, this girl's smell was boring. I'm out of here.

After the girl, I followed each of the other members. First just a few steps with the boy, then the dad, but the most was with the woman. Her smell was the absolute best. I galloped with my tiny legs following her into a soft, comfy, carpeted room where I took a quick break and enjoyed the comfort the strands of the carpet provided.

To my dismay, she soon left. And, pretty soon, I got up, too. There was no one there, just light to fill the empty space.

I crawled, passing the doorway and the staircase all the way to the main living room as the family called it. The kids were reaching for the bag that had smelled familiar before and suddenly, I knew why. That was my bag. It was the bag that held my almost scrumptious food and those delightful treats. I thought that I was being given food, but the family skipped straight to the dessert.

"Cody already has had his dinner. Just give him a treat," one of them had said. The only part I picked up was my name in that confusing sentence.

But, the boy reached for the treat box and pulled out a treat from it. He hurried over to the tile floor of the kitchen, and set the piece of tasty *gold* down. My mouth couldn't wait to eat the treat, but I needed a proper surrounding; I needed the feeling of comfort and luxury combined. So, I grabbed the treat and crawled over to the carpet, laying down all four feet against the smooth surface of the rug. In the distance, I heard the voices of the family. "He's taking it to the carpet again. Just like last time!" one said.

"It's okay," another replied.

With not another second to waste, I picked the treat up and gobbled it, ignoring their whines. I felt it flow down into my stomach where I felt a pleasant sensation. It was almost like a dance in my stomach.

Wait a minute. Just wait a minute. I've had this feeling before. And it was not at my own house; it was somewhere else. I can remember some other place where I had eaten a treat in an open, comfy space surrounded by other people with the same pleasant sensation. But, of course, I couldn't where.

"Paxton, come on," the girl in the family said. Paxton? Was that the boy's name? I'm not sure how, but it's not a foreign term to my mind. I remember this name or I think I can, but again, I can't remember from where. My brain is horrible at remembering past moments. Right now, storm clouds are circling my brain and I keep having these quick flashes of memories, but I can't place their details.

My eyes darted back and forth to the walls that were different from the ones in our house. And, seeing this, more clouds formed in my brain, fogging up my knowledge.

However, the clouds stopped. I made them stop. I began to create a path of sunshine for me before I followed the faded scent of my family at the door, leading to a path of tears instead. I approached the edge of the door and stuck my face in the small opening. But, my family wasn't there, and their scent was starting to disappear with each passing second.

Luckily for me, there was another rug by the door. It was not as comfy as the large one in the living room, but I could make do with it. I lowered my head towards the ground, my peripheral vision seeing the approaching feet of the family but my eyes only targeted the wooden planks.

Like lightning, my head jumped up. I felt another memory just zap through my brain. It was just a flash, but I had seen these wooden planks on the floor somewhere. Somewhere that seemed the same as now.

But, I can fight the lightning and the storm clouds. I can ignore these memories because they are ridiculous. I haven't been here before. I must just be remembering moments from somewhere else that are almost the same as now. So, in response to this, my head resumed back to its spot, but my eyes turned away from the wooden floor in front of me. Instead, they faced the blurry design of the rug I was laying on. Afterall, there was nothing familiar about the rug.

A little time passed before I got bored of sitting on the rug. I headed for the more comfier area in the living room where I had my treat before. I could smell the exact spot where I had gobbled it up, and that didn't make it any better. However, I still sat by the family's feet as they all plopped down on the couch there. To my luck, there was something amazing there. In each of the family member's hands, there was a round plate with food on it. And it smelled amazing: like a symphony of smells. My legs carried me closer to their feet where I stared right at them. And, they stared right down at me. I waited and waited. But, I wasn't given any food. I even gave the best puppy look I could, but they were not prone to the charms of cute me.

They were mean. Well, in the sense that they didn't give me any of their human food. My own family never gives me their own food either, but it's not like they try to act innocent, petting me or attempting to cuddle me in the end.

Pretty soon, the parents made their way to another room. They walked across the wooden hallway and disappeared at a turn; I was left with the two children. Paxton and someone else. Someone else who I had followed until she took a horrible bath and whose identity remains unknown.

The two children patted me a few times. I soon got bored sitting on the ground, so I got ready on my hind legs to jump onto the sofa. As I did, I settled down right near the girl. She just seemed friendlier, less smelly, and warm. She also gave me such soothing pats before turning her attention to a large screen in front of her.

Light was emanating from the screen and so many different shapes surfaced on it with loud sounds creeping around me. Seeing and hearing this reminded me of the large screen in my own home, similar to this. However, it also reminded me of something else.

I began to have the strangest sense of deja vu. I had seen this same large screen before, and it was not in my own home. And, I could almost recall feeling like this — resting upon a partially rough and comfy surface, next to someone, near a large cushion.

Have I been here before? That was the only question that could pop up in my head now. Why do I keep receiving all these strange flashes of memory from this house? Why do I remember this boy and maybe the girl?

As of right now, I wasn't sure if I should grow comfortable here or ignore whatever I was perceiving. Afterall, was I really sure that my family would come back? Was I sure that they'd come crawling through the door with their sudden hugs and chatter? Or, was I leaning towards the option where maybe they had given me off without a goodbye — well one goodbye from Sarah. But, to make it all worse, I could so deeply remember feeling this way surrounded by yellow walls — the color of these walls — a wooden floor, and four strangers. Or, maybe, I had felt this way before when I was dropped off at the horrible dog shelter. Honestly, I had no idea. I thought of several questions, but couldn't come up with the answers.

***

Some time later, I figured it was time for the family to s

sleep. The screen stopped spitting out light and those booming sounds came to an end. Thank god! Only, I am not thankful for the threat that I spotted outside just disappear without me tailing after it. It was a sound so startling and a weird sensation that I had to follow it. But, of course, despite my valiant efforts trying to save the kids, they just kept begging me to go back to them.

The mother came into the living room after a while and the kids followed her through the wooden hallway and with a sharp turn, up the stairs. I followed them, *kind of* eager to explore the rest of the house. Also, I really needed to clear out these stupid memories.

First, the kids went to their bathroom and stuck these long tubes with a brush on it in their mouths. After, they went to a room with striped walls. There, they wandered around the room before settling under the covers of their bed.

I settled on the comfy carpet in the room. My bottom on the carpet, and my legs stretched out and rested — it felt nice. I caught the kids staring at me, and the mom's eyes looking at me. Her mouth seemed to be moving, but I was not familiar with alien language, so I ignored it. At that moment, the lights in the room turned off. I could still make out the bed and the kids, but everything went dark. The mom started out the door, and so I followed. It was better than staying in a dark room in the same position.

I followed her downstairs until I approached my bed in the same room she was in. It was near another large bed and on a comfy carpet. To be honest, I am really starting to enjoy the floors of this house.

Just as light erupted from another source — a screen in their room — I walked onto my bed, and my body lowered onto my legs. In a matter of seconds, my eyes closed and everything around me was pitch dark and silent. You couldn't even hear crickets; I was in sleep mode.

***

As soon as the sun rose, my eyes peeked open. I climbed out of bed with my collar shifting from side to side. I can't believe they forgot to take off my collar — it ached.

I turned to my right, finding the woman snoozing on the right side of the large bed behind me. One of her hands was extended, and hanging off of the bed. The other was wrapped around her face, and her eyes could be barely seen. I took a small jump towards her hand, but the bed was too high up for me. So, I wandered over to the other side of the bed.

There was the man from yesterday who had greeted my family. He hadn't really interacted with me yet besides me following him, but I guess it wasn't his fault; I just never gave him a chance to pet me.

His eyes were covered with a dark fabric, but his arms lay on the side. He had his blanket pulled up to his neck.

I was just staring at his face and him laying there, restfully and peacefully, until a sound startled me.

It came from my left. Immediately, the man's hand removed the black fabric over his eyes and reached for the

178

device that made the sound. His hands extended towards a small rectangular thing and his finger tapped something on it. In just a millisecond, the sound stopped. Phew! Thank god. That sound was annoying and to be honest, scary.

At that moment, I thought that the sound might've woken him up, but in the middle of my celebration, the man pulled the fabric over his eyes and turned to the other side.

***

I had to wait a while until the man woke up. A few startling sounds later from the rectangle device, he finally mustered the courage to lift up from the bed and use his bathroom.

After sticking tubes and splashing water in his mouth and on his face, he left the bedroom. I followed him outside the room to the kitchen with the cold, tile floor. Pouring food into my food bowl, he stared at me for a few seconds while I gobbled up the food. Then, after rummaging through stuff in the kitchen, he grabbed my leash, fastened it on me, and we headed outside into the chilly, morning air.

I saw him carrying a plastic bag, the reason unknown, as he brought me along mailboxes and down the sidewalk. After smelling several corners of the sidewalk, I finally found the spot that wasn't the territory of another dog. Then, I did my business and continued walking.

Pretty soon, the man used the plastic bag to pick up

something. As I stared at him curiously at his actions, he pulled my leash and we went in the opposite way we came. I, less excited about going the same way, was forced to follow him as we made our way to his house. *The* house, with its floor being the only positive thing about it.

As we came inside and my leash was taken off, I wandered around the house and eventually settled on the carpet in the living room. I licked my paw and scratched my ear before time passed. I followed the father upstairs to the same room where I had been at last night. There were the two kids on the bed, snoozing in awkward positions. As I saw their faces, I leapt onto the bed and gave a lick to each of them. With just a one-eyed squint at me, they whined and turned to the other side. A failed mission for me.

I followed their constantly turning heads and walked across their bodies. One of them reached over to pet me, and the other remained with her eyes completely closed and her hand under her face.

And, suddenly, the moments came back. Moments from my house, not this place or somewhere else I was mistakenly thinking of. From my tiny, comfortable bed, I would walk with windows surrounding me as the sun rose. I would leap onto Sarah's bed, then Max's, and try to get their beautiful eyes to open. But, I would fail. Just like I am failing right now.

So, just like those times, I gave up right now. What did I care about these children anyways? I hopped off the bed and galloped all the way down the stairs until I touched the cold wooden floor of the house, my least favorite feeling.

***

The kids woke up after a little while. I sat on the carpet of the living room floor, much warmer than the cold wooden floor I had touched on my way down the stairs.

I heard a sneeze as the kids stomped a little bit quieter than is called a stomp and made their way downstairs to the peaceful living room. They plopped onto the couch with their hands holding something rectangular made of paper on which they would keep their eyes focused for the next half hour. I lay there, staring at their faces as they would sometimes turn to me with a begging arm motion. But, I continued to lay there, on the soft carpet. Did I mention that the floors in this house rock? Yup, I did.

As I continued to enjoy the comfort the carpet was providing to my furry body, I elapsed into a deja vu moment again. It was the carpet's fault. It was the carpet that I was enjoying that was now spooking me. I don't know why I never felt this after sitting here last night, but I felt it now. The sense of familiarity. I had sat on this carpet, I had laid on this carpet, and I had smelled and seen this carpet. The children's motions towards me also helped some memories to flourish. They would lay on their stomachs and stare at me straight in the eye and would sit down right next to me and give a pat. They motioned for me to come to them several times, and I could recall these

181

exact actions. Or I think I could. With my brain, nothing was guaranteed.

Only then, I heard the name that allowed me to remember everything.

It was the teenage girl who went up to her mother and asked, "Mom, can I give Cody his food?"

"Sure, go ahead, Sandra."

Sandra. Sandra. Sandra. So similar to Sarah. And then, through all the hints, through all the foggy memories, finally everything clicked together.

The storm clouds are gone, I am saved from being clueless, and I've just realized the real beauty of this home.

I was here. I was here a few months ago, in the summer. My family had abandoned me at that time without even a goodbye. I was left on the wooden floor of this house, on the comfy carpet in the living room, under the parents' bed, and in Sandra's room. This was the Johnsons' house. It was the place where I found my solitude, comfort, and enjoyment during that dark week without my family. And, those thrilling, most beautiful memories are coming back to me — such a nice dessert for my brain after all the confusion before.

I couldn't help but think now: will I have fun this time, too? Everything looks so promising, so inviting, and I'm eager to explore it all over again. But, something else comes in the way. The critical question of *will my family come back? Will they come back like last time or is this truly permanent?*

Something was wrong. I was starting to see each of the family members less. Especially Sandra. I hadn't witnessed her wide smile and long hair in a while. Usually, she would roam downstairs, but now, there was simply no Sandra downstairs. Just an empty jug of water and the constant footsteps of the mother going up and down the stairs usually carrying something. In fact, she was the only one I really saw. Like last time, the man was trapped behind something gray that also emanated a lot of light, and well, who knew where Paxton was?

Right now, the only word that crossed my mind was Sandra's name. Where was she? Why isn't she downstairs, comforting me and petting me?

Pretty soon, Paxton appeared and sat down on the couch he had left earlier.

He stayed there the entire time, doing whatever incomprehensible thing his hands were doing. A part of me was dreading being alone with him after my experience with him the last time I came here.

I remember how I used to start daydreaming of being in a pile of a thousand, no a million, beef jerkys and surrounded by endless amounts of meat and cheese. It was indeed a luxury. But, every time I would come back to life because of just how unique (we can put it that way) his touch was.

***

As I sat on the carpet staring at Paxton's messy hair, I suddenly realized what was going to be my new mission. I had daydreamed enough about beautiful sights of meat and relaxation while Sandra was nowhere to be found. *I* was going to find her.

So, with her scent nowhere to be discovered downstairs, I hopped onto the staircase and made my way up. *Bump, stomp, tap, bump, stomp...*

I reached the second floor of the house and peered at the walls. They were plain except for some human faces, none of which I recognized except for the parents.

I turned away from the faces and looked at the empty hallway with carpet and lifeless objects. I didn't know if it was simply cold air or if it was the emptiness inside of me, but right there, I felt cold. Nonetheless, I continued on. I needed to find Sandra.

I walked across the cold, carpeted hallway until I came across a blue room in front of me that was completely empty except for a huge bed two times taller than a normal bed and other miscellaneous items.

I soon left the room, and on my left, I found a door. It was weird how mostly every door in the house was open except this one. I approached it, gave a slight push with my body, and it opened.

And, what it revealed was magnificent.

It was the same striped room from the night before. It was the room where the two kids slept and where I had been before sleeping myself. Only now, it had Sandra. And she was laying in bed.

I turned to look at her face as she caught me in her room. She smiled and held out her hand for me to come. So, I did. I approached her bed and got ready to jump. In just one second, I had hopped onto her bed and she immediately started to pet me.

I could feel the warmth of her hand, but there was also something shaky about it. In fact, as my legs tried to step on hers, I felt a vibe from her. I could sense something was odd. She wasn't her usual kind, warm self, but someone else. And, she seemed weak.

Her eyes seemed fine, but her skin felt pale, and her body was shaking. She yawned a couple of times, and pretty soon, her eyes closed and she fell asleep.

But, there I was, resting with her. First of all, I had nothing else to do, and I couldn't leave Sandra by herself. She needed me.

***

I spent the night on her bed — being with her as much time as I could before I feeling bored and hopping off. I would walk around the home a little, sniff the mom, spend the least amount of time with Paxton, and earn a few minutes with the dad before jumping back onto Sandra's bed and staying with her all over again.

Finally, after a week, Sandra got out of bed. She came down the stairs as if wings had sprouted out of her arms, her legs taking off across the house, as if soaring. Actually, this was simply my imagination, but this could've been happening.

I was there when Sandra came downstairs. She was smiling again. Her weakness had flown away, her legs had regained their full strength.

In the following days, new memories were created. We went out for walks, the family laughed when I marked my territory, I chased other dogs, I even chased a squirrel, and I curled up with the family to receive their soothing pats.

All was good. All was promising, and everything was peaceful. Well, it was before my real family knocked on the door and I jumped into their arms.

Just like last time, I immediately lost the thought of the Johnsons when I hurried into my family's hands and into their amazing car.

But, something *was* different. Because now, even though I may forget, the memory of the Johnsons' home would remain. And, next time, if I ever came here all over again, my brain wouldn't have to dig that much or suffer through clouds of confusion, because I would recall everything right away.

Afterall, the Johnsons were the same, sweet family. And this was the same, sweet home. It was the same, beautiful home as last time. Caring, thrilling, safe, and amazing.

The Choice I Make

Make

- a very short story

My heart was beating fast. My mind was racing, my hands were shaking and fiddling; amid this all, a drop of sweat ran down my face every beating second. I was surely in panic mode, unsure of what to do about the situation in front of me. As the protector of Nafaria City, I was supposed to protect the people in it. Hence, the name protector. But, I had gotten myself into a difficult decision.

Here I was hesitating at the sight ahead of me. It was my friend, shaking in terror as one of the evil superhumans in our city grasped her by the neck. But to the side, there was a baby on the ground, her butt touching the rough concrete where her mother had fallen unconscious. Right behind the baby's beefy little arms and shrieking cries, the evil superhuman's sidekick was lurking about, probably getting ready to destroy the tiny human's life.

I was given extraordinary abilities — well, just one. Invisibility. Although it wasn't much, it was better than not having anything at all. And, because of the amazing person that I am, I put it forth towards a useful purpose: saving the city. But, even with my invisibility powers, I wouldn't be able to save both humans except hide from the superhumans. Just as I'd be running every ounce I have to grab one person, the superhuman at the same time could kill the other. No, the only way out of this situation is picking one. Only, I don't know which one.

Who do I help? The innocent baby or my innocent

friend who's been nothing but kind since I've moved to this city? My heart beats, pumping out blood to every part of my body, but I think it misses my thirsty brain. I'm completely blank. My eyes keep darting back and forth at the two humans, my mouth just wants to shout, but my brain wants to hide in the dark corner just when I need it the most.

My fingers were shaking. I think I was having a stroke. Even my head was feeling faint because I couldn't decide who to pick. I just wanted to cry right there. Or run away. Just hide in a bush and let both humans get slaughtered. But, I can't do that. If I can save one, then one I shall save. But, which one?

Which one? Which one? Which one? The innocent baby or my innocent friend? The baby who has a hopeful 100 years left to live, or my friend who has less time but is still a lot and deserves it. Maybe, I should save my friend. I don't know the baby, I don't know the mom; however, if I grab my friend, hurry away to another country, then I can block my ears from the horrible sensation of a baby decapitated and a woman left suffering. But, will I ever be able to face another baby and a mom again? Will I ever be able to look into the product of God right into the eyes and not cry or not want to live anymore? No, I can't pick my friend. But, if I save the baby, my friend's gone, and I'm left suffering through the halls of high school, all alone. Friendless. Unhappy.

My heart thumps in my chest like the rhythm of a drum. My brain is still static. My hands are ready to grab, but my fingers shake like I'm having a seizure. Why did I need to have invisibility? Why couldn't I get super speed? If I had the power to run at a million miles per hour, I'd be far away from here with everyone safe in their homes.

My mind, now suddenly awake, went back to the moment when it all happened. When I got the power which was limiting me here. When the alien glass from the UFO found its way into my apartment and pierced my foot. Blood had seeped onto the floor, but the supernatural remains of an alien planet seeped into my bloodstream, causing me to get the ability of invisibility.

I had fainted. My brain had failed for a few hours before I woke up in a hospital and turned out fine. Except for a tingly body, an alien bloodstream, and a selfish heart.

I have to admit, I wasn't very impactful or amazing or selfless like I have evolved into now. In reality, I was a thief. A sixteen year old thief. I had the perfect family, the perfect life before it was all taken away by a rash driver. Faster than I could blink, I was sent to a horrible foster home which I ran away from and landed in Nafaria City. Where I met her, my best friend. It was her purity, it was the perfection and light she saw in the world that made me want to keep the world she imagined safe. So, although difficult at first to just catch a few robbers and car thieves, I boosted my confidence and became a superhero. Until, some psycho doctor put the pieces of the glass in other humans to make them superhumans. But instead of turning them good like me, they became evil. It's so easy to corrupt people. And now, they're in front of me, about to kill the two people whom I can't decide between so that I pick one and become evil myself. Mission accomplished for them.

It would be easy if I were the person that long ago, but because of my friend, I am left here fiddling with the decision.

"Scarletttt. Hurry up. Show yourself and surrender or *both* of these people die." *Surrender.* The word stung me like a wasp would. Surrender, it would be the easiest decision in my predicament right now, but if I did, they would just kill me, and Nafaria would be left without a protector. No, I had to decide right here and then who to save.

Only one person was coming out alive. I knew that. I'd have to live with it. I'd have the image of blood, of guilt, of me leaving the area with one human dead, but I would just have to live with it. I managed to live with my parents gone, but it was my friend who helped me. My friend, my confidant, the piece of light in my life.

The only thing I can change is who I can live without. Will I be able to continue on my possibly immortal life of being unable to stare at babies and their mothers cuddling with them on any park bench? Will I be forever lonely and abandoned, knowing I'm the reason my best friend was murdered, someone who was innocent and the kindest person the Earth could offer?

I didn't have much time. Time kept going by every beating second with the evil superhuman and his sidekick surrounding my friend and the baby. "Well, then, Scarlet. If you're not going to show yourself, then I'll kill both of them."

And then time froze. It froze for me. I couldn't breathe anymore. My lungs snapped close for a moment while my legs got ready to run. And then my body started functioning again when I hurried to a rock and threw it as hard as I could towards what might have been the worst choice I could make right now. It zapped through the air, its irregular edges beating the wind and making its way to the chest of the evil superhuman. With all my adrenaline placed in the throw — at that moment, I wished I had super strength — it pierced the skin of the superhuman, probably making its way into his heart. With a slight shake, a sound of pain, the superhuman fell to the floor. I don't think that killed him, but until the rock makes it way out of his heart, he won't be getting up again.

I was about to celebrate when uncontrolled energy from the superhuman erupted into the air and fell because of gravity towards where he was. Where my friend was. Where the baby was nearby. And with a scream, with another boost of adrenaline, I ran towards where the energy was hurtling just as a weapon landed in my back and I fell to the ground. I was unsure of where the energy landed but completely sure that I was dead. I wasn't immortal.

All I could see was darkness. There was no sense of life, only me drowning in some abyss that is the feeling of death. And, that was why I made the worst choice possible. I think I killed everyone: the superhuman, the baby, the mom, my friend, and me. Nafaria's protector is gone and two innocent humans with her.

All seemed lost. All was lost. But, when I woke up in my bed, maybe all that was lost was the bedsheet. It had fallen to the floor, and I realized my legs were freezing.

I think I screamed. And, that's when my father ran in. My late father, who was apparently still alive.

He hurried in my room, sticking his arms out in consolation. "Scarlet! Are you okay?"

"What?" That was the only word that came out of my mouth. I stared at the blue walls surrounding and stared out my window at some unfamiliar land.

"I heard you scream. Are you okay?"

"Uh, yes. Yes, I am. I'm just freezing."

"Oh. The blanket fell on the floor, kiddo." He brought the blanket back on the bed and turned to leave. "Hey, kiddo."

"Yes?"

"The super speed isn't bothering you, right?"

"What?"

"The super speed. For your seventh birthday."

"I'm sorry, what?" I shrieked.

"Are you trippin' or something, sweety? On Nafaria, we get superpowers on our seventeenth birthday. You got super speed, something you always wanted."

"Oh, yeah. Right. Sorry, I am a little, uh, exhausted."

"Oh, that's fine. Go back to bed. Tomorrow, we'll test your superpowers out."

And, that's when I realized. I was an alien, not a human infected by alien glass. I was on the planet Nafaria, not Nafaria City, which was beautiful by the way, and my dream wasn't reality. At least, I hoped it would never be. I hoped that I would never have to make a choice like that ever again. And, now, with super speed, I doubt I will ever have to.

THE END

CPSIA information can be obtained
at www.ICGtesting.com
Printed in the USA
BVHW081053020721
611053BV00006B/220